Elfriede Jelinek was born in the Austrian alpine resort of Mürzzuschlag and grew up in Vienna, where she attended the famous Music Conservatory. The leading Austrian writer of her generation, her other works include *Wonderful, Wonderful Times*, *Women as Lovers*, and *The Piano Teacher*, now a prize winning film (all published by Serpent's Tail), as well as plays and essays. In 1986 she was awarded the Heinrich Böll prize for her contribution to German language literature, and in 1998 she received the prestigious Georg Büchner Prize for the entirety of her work. In 2004, she was awarded the Nobel Prize for Literature.

LUST

ELFRIEDE JELINEK

Translated by Michael Hulse

The translator would like to thank Martin Chalmers and Dorle Merkel for their helpful advice

Library of Congress Catalog Card Number: 91-61209

A complete catalogue record for this book can be obtained from the British Library on request

Originally published in German in 1989 by Rowohlt Verlag GmbH

First published in English in 1992 by Serpent's Tail

4 Blackstock Mews, London N4 2BT
website: www.serpentstail.com

Typeset by Contour Typesetters, Southall, Middlesex
Printed by Mackays of Chatham, plc

This translation received financial support from the Commission of the European Community, Brussels

10 9 8 7 6 5 4 3 2

LUST

_____

1

CURTAINS VEIL THE WOMAN in her house from the rest. Who also have their homes. Their holes. The poor creatures. Their hideaways, abideaways: their fixed abodes. Where their friendly faces abide. And all that distinguishes them is the one thing that's always the same. In this position they go to sleep: indicating their connections with the Direktor, who, breathing, is their eternal Father. This Man dispenses truth as readily as he breathes out air. That is how much his rule is taken for granted. Right now he has just about had it with women, so he says. See, there he is, yelling that all he needs is this woman. His woman. There he is, as unknowing as the trees all around. He is married. The fact acts as a counterbalance to his pleasures. This Man and his wife do not blush in each other's presence. They laugh. They have been in the past, are now and ever shall be all things to each other.

The winter sun is small at present. It is depressing an entire generation of young Europeans growing up around here or who come here for the skiing. The children of the workers at the paper mill: they might well recognize the world for what it is at six in the morning when they go to the cowshed and suddenly become strangers terrible to the animals. The woman goes for a walk with her child. She alone is worth more than half the bodies around here taken together. The other half work for the Man at the paper mill when the siren howls. And people keep a tight hold on what's closest, what's stretched out beneath them. The woman has a large clean head. She goes out walking with the child for a good hour, but the child, intoxicated with the light, would rather be rendered insensate, insensitive. By sport. The moment you take your eyes off him, he's plunging his little bones into the snow, making snowballs and throwing them. The ground gleams with blood. As if served up fresh. Torn birds' feathers on the snowy path. Some marten or cat has been going about its natural business, slinking about on all fours, and some creature or other has been gobbled up. The carcass has been dragged off. The woman was brought here from the town, to this place where her husband runs the paper mill. The Man is not counted one of the local people; he is the only one who counts. The blood spatters on the path.

The Man. He is a largish room where talking is still possible. His son too has to start learning to play the violin now. The Direktor does not know his workers as individuals. But he knows their total value as a work-force. Good day there, everybody! A works choir has been established. It is funded by donations. So the Direktor has something to keep him occupied. The choir travels everywhere in buses, so people can say, that's terrific. Often they have to take a stroll round little provincial towns. Off they go, with their unmeasured strides and their measureless wishes, gaping at the provincial shop windows. In the halls, the choir offers a front view of itself, its rear view turned to the bar. When you see a bird in flight, all you see is the underside, too. Taking deliberate, industrious strides the songbirds ooze forth from the hired bus, which is steaming with their dung, and promptly try out their voices in the sunshine. Clouds of song rise beneath the mantling sky as the prisoners are lined up.

Meanwhile their families are getting by without Father, on a small income. The Fathers eat sausages and drink beer and wine. They damage their voices and senses by using both without due care. A pity that they are of humble birth. An orchestra from Graz could take the place of every one of them. Or alternatively give them back-up. Depending what mood it was in. These awful feeble voices, cloaked in air and time. The Direktor

wants them to use their voices to beg for his benevolence.
Even the lowly have a chance with him if he notices that
they have musical talent. The choir is the Direktor's
hobby and is looked after accordingly. When they are not
being driven about the men are in their pens. The
Direktor invests his own money when it's a matter of the
bloody, stinking qualifying rounds in the regional
championship. He assures himself and his singers of
permanence, of continuation beyond the fleeting
moment. The men, built above-ground and still building,
still building. So that by their works shall their wives
know them when they are pensioned off. But at week-
ends these most divine of creatures come to a weak end:
they don't climb the scaffolding, they climb onto a dais at
the pub, and sing under compulsion, as if the dead might
return and applaud. The men want to be bigger, greater,
and lo, all their works and words want the same thing.
Edifying edifices.

At times the woman is dissatisfied with these defects
that burden her life: husband and son. The son a full-
colour copy, a perfect reproduction, a unique and photo-
graphable child. He runs along after Father so that he too
will be a man one day. And Father jabs the violin in
position under his chin so the foam well and truly sprays
from his teeth. With her life the woman answers for the
smooth running of their enterprise and for good feelings
each to each. Via this woman the Man has passed himself
on to perpetuity. The woman was of the best stock that
could be found and has passed herself on to the child. The
child is well-behaved, except at sports, where he is
allowed to run wild and needn't put up with anything
from his friends, who have unanimously chosen him as
the ladder to the heaven of full employment. His father
sees to it that he himself won't pass away from the earth.
He manages the factory and manages his memory,
rummaging in the pockets of memory for the names of
workmen who try to get out of singing in the choir. The

child is a good skier, the village children are like grass beneath him. There they stand beside their shoes. The woman in her daybag, which is washed out every day, no longer goes on stage, no, she provides the child with an anchorage on her blessed coast, but the child is forever running away, taking his fire off to the poor people who live in the little houses. Intending them to find his vivacity contagious. In his fine garb he will glide across the whole world. And Father is as puffed-up as a pig's bladder, he sings, plays, yells, fucks. The choir does as he wishes, roaming from valley to mountainside, from sausage to roast, singing likewise. Never asking what they're getting paid for doing it. But the choir members are never laid off. The house is so bright that it saves on lighting costs! Indeed, its brightness is better than light. And song makes a happy home.

The choir has just arrived. Older indigenous peoples out to escape their wives. Sometimes the wives are there too, their locks stiff (sacred power of hairdressers in the country, salting these beautiful women with great pinches of permanent waves!), they have alighted from the vehicles and are having a nice day out. The choir, after all, cannot simply sing to light and air. Calmly the wife of the Direktor walks to the front on Sundays. In the village church. Where God, the mere sight of whom in pictures is an outrage, talks to her. The old women kneeling there already know what lies ahead. They know how it all ends. But still they haven't managed to find the time to learn a single thing. They work their way round from station to station of the cross, and for what? So that soon they can meet their maker, the Lord God Almighty, that hallowed member of the trinity of airhead godhead, face to face. Their slack-skinned bellies in their hands to prove their worthiness to be received. At last, time stands still. Hearing breaks loose of the detritus of a lifetime's perception of their lot. Nature is beautiful in a park and so is singing in an inn.

Amidst all these surrounding massifs to which athletes come the woman realizes that there is no stable centre in her life, not even a recreation centre where a life of recreation might be waiting. The family can do good. But it expects to eat good food too. And to bag the quarry on feast-days. The loved ones are so fond of Mother. There they all sit, together, blissful. The woman talks to her son (bacon infested with the maggots of love) and fills him with her all-pervasive low and tender shrieking. She is concerned about him. Protects him with her soft weapons. Every day he seems to die a little more, the older he becomes. The son takes no pleasure in Mother's griping and promptly demands a present. Brief transactions such as these, transactions involving toys or sports equipment, are their way of trying to communicate. Lovingly she flings herself on her son, but even as a torrent she simply flows away, to be heard somewhere far beneath him, in the depths. And she has only this one child. Her husband comes in from the office and instantly she hugs her body in tight so that the Man's senses will not scent a bit of what they fancy. Music sounds forth, straight out of the baroque era and the record player. Imperative: to resemble the full-colour holiday snaps as closely as possible. Not to change, from one year to the next. There isn't a single truthful word in this child, I swear; all he wants is to be off skiing, you take it from me.

Outside feeding times, the son talks very little to his mother, even though she beseechingly pulls an intimate blanket of food up over the two of them. Mother tempts the child out for a walk. And ends up paying dearly, by the minute. Listening to this neatly-turned-out child talking like a television. Which is his main source of nutrition. Off he goes now, out for a walk, unfearing, because he hasn't been watching the nastiness of the videos yet today. At times the sons of the mountains are already asleep at eight in the evening, while the Direktor is adeptly filling more art into his engine. And what most puissant of voices is it, pray, that bids the herds in the meadow be upstanding, each and every one? And likewise the poor and weary early in the mornings when they look across to the opposite bank where the rich have their holiday homes? I think it's called Ö3 Wecker. Playing one hit after another from six a.m., those busy little rodents, gnawing away our days from the moment we wake.

In the Hitlerian back rooms at the gas stations they are taking a swipe at each other again, the petty people tied up in apron strings, wasting themselves and their half portions of ice cream beneath colourful umbrellas. It is always over so quickly. And work takes so long and the rocks endure for ages. No matter how endlessly they go on repeating themselves, all these people can do is reproduce. The hungry mob. Yanking its sex out of that door so conveniently positioned up front. These people don't have windows, so that they don't have to look at their partners when they're at it. We are kept like cattle! And there we go, worrying about getting on in the world!

On the ground lie peaceful paths. In the family there is always one who is waiting in vain, or falling in the struggle to stake a claim. Mother's labours afford her a sense of security, which the fruit of her labour, bent over his instrument, promptly destroys. The local people don't feel at home here, they have to retire for the night when evening life awakens good and proper in the sporting people. To them the day belongs, to them the night belongs as well. Mother monitors the child, squatting on the wall where she lives, so the child does not feel too comfortable about things. This violin doesn't particularly care for the child. In the catalogues, all the like-thinking crowd stride out defiantly, intending to fill each other's cups to overflowing. The personal column is read, and each person rejoices in his own little night, cast into the dark of an unfamiliar body. The diligent carpenters of life put ads in the papers, hoping to install their partition walls in other people's dark corners. One man on his own ought not to be too much for himself to handle! The Direktor reads the ads and places an order for his wife so that he can order her to her place, which is in red nylon lace with holes in the silence for the stars to peep through. One woman isn't enough for the Man. But the threat of disease restrains him. Prevents him from putting forth his sting and supping honey. One day he will forget that his sex can be the end of him and he will demand his share in the great harvest. We want to have fun! We want to ramify! The people who placed the ads lie in complicated positions on their mattresses, describing the paths along which they dally. It's to be hoped their fires don't go out; that would mean they would have to go out themselves and court disappointment. His wife is not enough for the Direktor, but still, he's a public figure, and he has to make do with this small car. He tries to make the best of it: to live and be loved. The children of people who're there to be used: they themselves are employees in the paper mill (it is a temptation to them, the unbound product of which bound books are made), they are unlovely to look at. It takes a siren howling at them to produce any sign of life. At the same time they are hurled out of life and fall like cataracts, superfluous, from the lofty heights of their savings. The helm has already been seized from their hands and in their stead their wives are making for the safe harbour which the men were at such pains to avoid and to void. They are the fruit of dry vines, shrivelled and rotten in no time at all. On their mattresses they are overcome by the desire for death. Their wives die by their own hand (or have to be given a helping hand by the state). They are not private. They do not have anywhere beautiful to live. What you see of them is what you get. What you see, and what you sometimes hear coming from the choir. Nothing good. They can do a lot of things at the same time and yet they still don't ripple the water in the pool where the Direktor's wife in her swimsuit stretches out on her blanket. The blanket coverage of Nature. Nature, immeasurably high and remote from us average consumers.

The water is blue and never takes a rest. But still the Man returns from his day's work to his home. Not everyone can have taste. The child has a lesson this afternoon. The Direktor has put everything on computer. He writes the programmes himself by way of a hobby. He has no love of the wild; the silent forest means nothing to him. The woman opens the door, and he perceives that there is nothing so big but he will be master of it, but neither must it be too small or else it'll be opened up immediately. His greed is an honest thing. It fits him just as the violin fits under the child's chin. These dear people encounter each other frequently in the house, for everything comes from their hearts and is proclaimed unto the light. The Man wants to be alone with his divine wife now. Poor folk have to pay before they can put in to shore.

Now the woman doesn't even have time to lower her gaze. The Direktor has other ideas when she makes to go into the kitchen to fix something up. He takes her arm in a determined grip. First he wants a crack at her. He's cancelled two appointments in order to have it. The woman opens her mouth to cancel *this* appointment, but she thinks of his strength and shuts her mouth again. This Man would play his tune even in the bosom of the mountains, his violin stroke would echo off the rocks, he'd stroke his rocks off. Time and again the same old song. This resounding banging tune. So astoundingly terrible. To the accompaniment of resentful looks. The

woman hasn't the heart to refuse herself. She's defence-
less. The Man is perpetually ready to go. Greedy for his
pleasure. To pleasure himself. Lo, this happy day is there
for the rich and the poor, but unfortunately the poor
begrudge it the rich. The woman laughs nervously as the
Man, still wearing his coat, deliberately exposes himself
to her. And there it is, the thick-headed thick head and
shaft of his member. The woman's laughter grows
louder and she slaps herself on the mouth, startled. She's
threatened with a beating. Her head is still full of music,
Johann Sebastian Bach, expressing her own feelings and
those of others, music guaranteed to give pleasure, going
round and round in circles on the record player, chasing
its tail. The Man is chasing his tail too, or his tail is
chasing and he is following. So it goes with men, ever
onwards, their works ever greater but presently collapsing behind their backs. The trees in the forest are more
stoutly and reliably upstanding. Calmly the Direktor
chats about her cunt. How he will force it open in a
moment. He seems intoxicated. His words totter and
reel. He grips the woman's hip in his left hand and yanks
her serviceable (easy to service her) clothing up over her
head. She wriggles in his heavy-weight presence. He
yells at her for wearing tights, which he long since
forbade her to wear, stockings are more feminine and
make better use of the available holes, if they don't
indeed create new ones. He tells the woman he is going
to have her real good now. Twice. At least. Women are
planted full of hopes and live off memory, but men live
off the moment, which belongs to them and, when
carefully tended, can be gathered into a little heap of time
which likewise belongs to them. At night they have to
sleep and can't fill up. They are afire and warm up in
small containers. Surprise surprise, this woman has been
secretly rendered infertile through pills; the Man's
never-becalmed heart would not countenance having no
life gush forth from his ever brimful tank.

*

Beside the woman, clothing falls in a heap, like dead animals. The Man, still in his coat, is standing with his member standing firm amidst the folds of his clothing. Like light falling on a stone. The tights and panties make a moist ring around the woman's slippers as she steps out of them. Happiness seems to be making the woman go slack. She can't grasp it. The Direktor's cumbrous cranium worries amongst her pubic hair, he bites, his desire is always at the ready, ready to desire something of her. He raises his head to the air and now presses hers to the neck of his bottle, here, taste this. Her legs are in a tight grip. He is touching her up. He cracks her skull on his prick, vanishes inside her and gives her derrière a good hard pinch to help things along. He forces her head back so that her neck cracks, an ungainly sound, and he slurps at her labia, gripped and gathered tight, the life gazing silently from his eyes up to her. Patience: the fruit'll ripen yet. That's what you get if you stack your human habits one atop the other to pick something off the top of the tree, only to find you don't like the taste after all. Everything is hampered and trammelled by the bans and banns of lust and desire. Even on a low hill there's a limit to how much will grow, and the limits placed on us are rigid and extend not much further than we can reach, and we can't reach far, not much of a voyage in our little blood vessels, hard and rigid.

The Man pushes on alone. But it can't be good for the woman to stay in this position for long. This position she has in his house. She wriggles and jiggles and has to open her legs somewhat. His teeth pluck at her belly regardless. The Man inhabits a living hell of his own, but there are times when he has to emerge from it and go down into the pastures. The woman resists, but her resistance is doubtless no more than an act, she is welcome to another slap or two if she wants, if she's set on denying the Man's soul its light. A fair amount has been drunk. The Direktor almost spends himself entirely in his expensive surroundings, in the gloom of which he rages about the food the woman cooks for him. She does not want to let him in. And he feels so big, as if he were all men in one. Just to unload a little here between the standard lamps would unburden him, after all, he has to bear the burden of many who do nothing but grow like the grass on the riverbank, stupid, never giving a thought to the morrow when they must get up. Hermann. Now, having lifted up his wife out of her shoes, he continues the uplifting experience by straddling her on the living room table. Anyone can look in, anyone can envy the rich the beautiful things they keep hidden away. She is flattened on the table and her breasts, big warm steaming cowpats of breasts, flop apart. The Man lifts his leg in his own garden and then off he goes and lifts it at every corner he comes to, too. Not even the haziest patch of ground is safe from him. It is as normal as erotic love, which has never started a fire in their dry wood, the dryness they are born to but do not want on any account to remain in. No, the Direktor will reply to small ads, to exchange his old Ford for a more up-to-date, more powerful model. If only it weren't for the fear of this most up-to-date of diseases, then there would never be silence in the workshops of the Lord. And in the home too there would be notices on the board: Desire, the white member (of a well-hung parliament). Mighty waves go crashing through Time, and mighty is the foaming desire of men, unceasingly. Far-off places are where they love to roam, but they'll also use what they've got at home. The woman wants to get away, to escape these reeking fetters. She has been drawn forth out of nothingness, out of the void, and every day the Man cancels her with his stamp anew, rendering her null and void. She is lost. Mechanically he flicks the woman's legs over him. Various objects belonging to the child fall off the table and bounce softly on the carpet. The Man is the one who still appreciates classical music. With one arm he reaches forwards and opens up the deck. There's a sound of music, the woman puts up with a good deal, mortals live on their wages and work, but, right, music really is an essential part of the experience. The Direktor's weight keeps the woman down. All he needs to keep down the workers, as they joyfully return from their labour to their leisure, is a signature, he doesn't have to lie upon them. And the sting that hangs by his testicles never sleeps. But in his breast his friends sleep, with whom he used to go to brothels. The woman is promised a new dress as the man rips off his coat and jacket. He is fighting the good fight against alcohol, his tie is twisted into a noose. If I could only have this clad in brand new words this minute! Underhand the Direktor has lit the stereo's fire, and now the music is racing off the turntable and setting the Direktor racing: pick-up arms move forward to play their part, and a Direktor has to get his end away! For his pleasure shall last till you can see the bottom and the poor, drained of love, are sent off the rails and have to take a ride to the labour exchange. For all things shall be everlasting and what's more they shall be indefinitely repeatable, so say the men, and they give a tug at the reins which Mummy once held in her loving hands. Of course you can, dear. And now the Man slides into his wife as if he were greased, in and then out again. Nature cannot have been mistaken about this field; we don't want anything else growing here. It is a community of flesh, and the farmers, who are quick to cry if they're not taken on to earn a little on the side, grow angry if their wives stroke the surprised cattle destined for the slaughter. With Death the gentlemen like to be on good terms, but business must go on as usual. And even unto the poorest shall gladly be accorded the daily pleasure of their women's embraces, where they can be Big Boys after 10 p.m. But for this Direktor time doesn't count, he doesn't have to clock on; after all, he manufactures time himself, and the cards are punched in till the clocks cry for mercy.

*

He bites the woman's breast, and her hands jerk
forward. This only excites him more, and he hits her on
the back of her head and tightens her grip on her hands,
his enemies of old. For his slaves he has no love either. He
stuffs his sex into the woman. The music races ahead and
their bodies race ahead as well. The Frau Direktor loses a
little of her control, the bulb's a little loose, better screw
it firmly in again. The Man is a sleeping dog that
shouldn't have been woken and fetched home from a
circle of business friends. He carries his weapon below
his belt. Right now he has fetched his pistol out; out it
has come like a shot. The woman is kissed. Spitting
words of love are slobbered in her ear. This flower
wasn't in full bloom for long, won't you thank it? Just
now he was wallowing and waltzing inside her, soon his
fingers will be producing a fine sound on the violin. Why
is the woman turning her head aside? In Nature's society
there is a place for every one of us! Even the smallest of
us, even the very least member, though it won't be in
great demand. This Man has emptied himself into the
woman, he wouldn't mind trying out naughtier tricks in
the pool some day! In the correct questionmark position
for diving, the Direktor withdraws from the woman,
leaving his waste behind. Presently she will be caught in
the trap of the household once more and will return
whence she came. It is a long while yet to sundown. The
Man has poured forth his joy and now, the slush
dribbling from his mouth and genitals, goes off to
cleanse himself of the day's toil.

The community looks up to them in all things. Let's face
it, it's a community short on sporting lasses to look up to.
The woman beds down in her troubles and Hermann
beds down on the woman, in the peace of the night. And
then their son: he has mastered the other children more
completely than his violin. Father manufactures the very
least of the things that pass beneath the flame of his
passion: paper. All that remains, wherever the eye looks

upon the works of men, is ash. The woman averts her gaze from the table she has laid, opens a hatch in her dress and tips the leftovers in, true unto herself. Today the family, *en famille*, is drinking in its own memories from the projector. The food is late, the boy is late, he messes it about terribly. He won't do a thing he's told, he isn't as good as gold. For months he's been promising to improve his violin playing, but Father finds it far more enjoyable to lavish blows on this friendly young creature. The whole country likes to be lavish. It lives on Art. But not all the good citizens and the faithful do so, and none would merit a Very Good in the tests.

The woman's tongue is a dress that covers everything. She absolves herself crunching the salted snacks that seem so much bigger on television than when the hosts dissolve to meaningless nothingness in the mouth. Still, we too, when our bodies are in an evening mood, tip the snacks into our very own personal sewage systems. Father bends over his son. Tender as sausage. Son is sure to get his BMX bike. The Direktor's son enjoys the village children's envy as one might enjoy a stiff pinch of power. Out he promptly goes into the open to smash something up. But the boy is Father's spoils, he spoils him: he has to bow his head over bow and violin today, so the sound that's produced can be used elsewhere to oil feelings. Father likes to show off his progenitorial profit at the instrument. And how Father makes use of this instrument, his child, as if the boy were a shell he had cast off! The boy's wrist has to be relaxed and flexible, it's better for trade, and with the delicate bow he shall roam to and fro in the pastures of the immortals, the family of the great, who are all to be restored to life with great, familiar, restorative sounds. Such horrid sounds, too! Jagged Mozart, if you're in luck. And if you've been tied down by the ankles to prevent you from wandering far afield to graze in other pastures.

*

The banks offer shoulder-bags in an attempt to win the custom of the very young. Even this riff-raff, the mere protégés of parents, want accounts of their own; there's no accounting for it. In a year or so the money will be looking good: it'll be a car, for death on the roads, or a furnished apartment, for death in your own four walls. Always assuming that — like the Direktor's son — you are a child under fourteen, guiltless, single, alive, but already singled out for a life among the clientèle, the future consumer guild that will tax their hearts with the wish — consume their souls with the desire — to have some gilt-edged value added. Perhaps some of us are destined to be clerks behind counters, for what are all these benches doing here anyway? The boy, scarcely baked through, dashes out into the biting cold. He has to take the healing plunge and cool off. He has to listen to the cries of his people, so that he will know how to make them cry all the more.

The Man, having shaved for the second time that day, returns to ride the woman like a boat before his flood. Her hills and valleys plus branches etc. offer prospects of plenty, true, but that final perfection conferred by degradation is still lacking. The Man, buoyed up on the breeze, creates the woman. He draws her parting and tosses her legs apart as if her bones had wilted. He beholds God's tectonic faults on her thighs, they do not bother him, he goes climbing in his private mountains taking a safe path that he knows well. He knows every step along the way. How should he fall? It is his own house. And who indeed would not wish to hang his hat on a peg of his own? Property imposes no duties on the owner; it merely prompts envy in his rivals. Years ago, in the Book of Life, this woman shifted into reverse. What can she still be expecting? He reaches under her skirt and batters through the walls of underwear. He wants to force his way into his wife (this is just a family affair) so that he will sense where his limits are. I rather think he would burst his banks, if it weren't that he's rudderless. He'd be giddy, up there on his own path. All in all, men would quite stand over us if we didn't enclose them within us from time to time, till they are tiny and quiet and quite surrounded. Now the woman involuntarily sticks out her tongue, and why? Because the Direktor has activated a muscle in her jaw, by means of which a snake could spit venom any time, it only needs to be shown how. The Man leads her into the bathroom, giving her his non-stop line of reassuring patter, and bends her over the edge of the tub. He fumbles in her undergrowth. So that he can get in at last without having to wait for the night. He parts her foliage and branches. The tatters of her dress are ripped off. Hair falls into the plughole. Her behind gets a good hiding: where can she be hiding? Where else but behind these gates, which the howling mob will storm and breach at last, the whole amiable crowd of consumers and foodstuff-of-life manufacturers shoving forward to the buffet. Here we are. Our services are required. The woman is offered an organ of similar design or of similar value. He'll screw the ass off her, it's all he wants in life, except to screw the rest of the world and draw his massive monthly salary. A shudder goes through him and he spends his entire sum, far more than any money he could make; how should the woman not be touched by this ray of annunciation? Now she contains the whole man and nothing but the man, as much as she can take; and he maintains the woman, as long as he finds her interior and wallpapering pleasing. He shifts her forequarters into the bathtub. As the proprietor of these and similar premises, he throws her back room open. No client, only he himself, can let in so much fresh air. No one but the Direktor can rain down on her like this. In a short while, with a yell, he will have relieved himself, this enormous horse, eyes rolling, foaming at the mouth, driving the cart right into the dirt. The woman's car is not there for her to drive wherever she may please; he has already shown her the route she is to take, shooting a track clear through the forest for her.

The woman clumsily kicks her slipper heel out, kicking at this clumsy heel who's slipped inside her. She's heard his private parts slapping like a harvester against the rim of the bath. The kick enrages him. The shit will be sticking to him, what a life. A wily lot, the weaker sex. At pains to look beautiful into the bargain. The Man resolves to command the woman to observe their marriage contract. He claps his hand across her mouth, and is bitten, just a few percent of her jaw power, so he has to withdraw the hand in question. He covers the woman with night. But for her enlightenment and his own satisfaction, he shoves his electricity main up her arse. She tries to shake him off, but quickly tires and has to go through with it, eyes shut. He has no love of the wild. Being so wild himself. All about them is a yawning emptiness in the house: the only signs of life are the bushes of hair on his and her abdomen, a sign that says you can get it on tap right here. This year's wine every day of the year. Can't fool us. Awkward nothings are slobbered into the woman's warm earhole. The power of the Man! No need for trickery or weapons. She need only open the gate, for this is his dwelling place, and it's hard to keep back his seed. With a smile, the Creator brings forth out of men their product, so that it may grow accustomed to dashing about in our midst. The Man distributes Creation at a forceful pace, and meanwhile Time passes at a pace of its own. He smashes the tiling and glass in that shady room, which rejoices beneath his busy endeavours and in the brightness of his light. Only within the woman is it dark. He enters her arse and bangs her face against the edge of the bath. She cries out yet again. The pilot settles in for a lengthy session in his cockpit. He himself may already be at rest, but his cock is pitting itself against the elements, ever onward, cliff to crag.

Such a one dives into the shit as others dive into the sea: throwing the switch marked *blow* on his appliance, he goes on full throttle until he has totally emptied his dustbag.

2

LATER SHE CALLS FOR her son. Though not so long ago she felt replete with the dear image of her child, her one protective casing to guard against the groping Man, who holds her tighter than a customer holds the drink of his choice. He needs no protection for his sex, and his torrent pours down the nearest channel. The child knows a good deal about all this. The boy peeps grinning through the keyholes, spying out the joys of the home. The boy cops a sly, audacious eyeful of Mother's body, having come in from the wilderness out there, the wilderness his comics call the Wonderland of Childhood. Is that smile on Mother's face adrift like a boat? Or has it been carved into her features? The child can't tell when he snuggles into the nest that Father built. They belong to each other, for the meat inspectors who crowd outside the fence. They even seek each other out, undirected as the potpourri of clouds up there in the purple sky. Not knowing why. Though perhaps they do know: the child has a hungry mouthful of dirty talk to be stopped, talk concerning his mother and the blood that frequently stains her panties. The child knows everything. He is white and his face is brown from the sun. In the evening he will be bathed. He will have prayed. He will have done his work. And he will cling to the woman, graze upon her, bite her nipples to punish her for allowing Father to explore her tunnels and piping. Are you listening? This is language itself, wanting to get a word in.

The miracle of travel is that one encounters an unfamiliar place and then flees it with a shudder. But if one has to remain together, a four-colour poor-quality reproduction of Nature, each belonging entirely to the other, a family, then you will find only the Pope, the kitchen and the Austrian People's Party to honour your work and to grant an indulgence for all the sins it has committed. The family, this vulture, keeps itself as a pet. The child never listens. There he sits with his secret playthings, which partly consist of disgusting pictures and partly of the original material for those pictures. Son contemplates his little tail. Often his gun is jammed. There the selfish kid squats with his private collection, almost human in his blabbering greed. The Pope has whole libraries of the stuff. Mealtime. As it enters his insensate maw, the Man praises the food his wife has prepared. Today she did the cooking herself! What happens on the plate reaches his place of residence, his address deep down in his gut, where it is tossed to and fro like an eaglet in the spinning air. This is the responsibility of the woman. Of women. The Man questions his wife with mute glances: time to bang the daylights out of her again? But the boy might hear if Father gets into the woman's yawning emptiness now, she tells him, hoping to get away with this excuse. But no: off she is promptly led, in obeisance to the Man's ludic lust. She clings on tight to the bedroom door, but the boundary line is the bathroom, one door further, where the limits have already been tested and exceeded today.

It all happens very quietly. Today, unusually, the Man has come home for lunch. Man takes his animal food from the pastures out there, and yet he does not recognize his four-legged friends when he finds them in the serving dish. At the last, the woman is required to undress. Now we've got more time. The child has been stuffed; it has to sit still at school. But for the woman to be preserved, she first has to plunge into the Man's foaming waves. The Man sees himself as a Noble Savage. Buying his meat at the woman's counter. The family is like a small business, a snack bar in the station. Quite alone, a manikin on one leg, for you can't rely on the second leg, the woman. The Man's claims to his own territory, the divine mountain paths where only he may go a-wandering, have already been registered with the

Austrian Women's Disaster Relief Group. A-frolicking he will go, aloft on the wondrous paths. But every evening at seven on the dot the mountains toss him back down to the eyrie of twigs he collected himself. His wife (he tells Nature with a smile, lying) is waiting. He has to go to lasso her in. He and she together constitute an association for life. A space tiny and bare as memory contains the whole of him. The woman does not die, verily she is created by the sex of the Man. Who has reconstructed a complete original scale model of her lower abdomen in his lab. How the Man loves making his appearances, a body straight from the freezer, thawing as fast as he can!

While his parents, Father burning high as a turned-up flame, Mother a mere breath on a window pane, are at each other, the child is clacking the flap of the letter-box, bored. This winter the school bus occasionally gets stuck in the deep snow. The children, who have cosy homes waiting for them, go hungry. That old knacker Nature forces them to capitulate (marvellous, really, that scourged, purged Nature can still make demands of us). They are put up for the night and read Mickey Mouse comics or other things their fathers haven't approved. They will get sausage in their sleeping bags and feel ill-accommodated. Even cars sometimes crack up in this cold. But we are warm, we are in safety, we are ready for the consecration, at last we are ready to be disillusioned by our partners. How glad we shall be! Till the manuals on life skills come to offer advice to us, in whom no one can live, telling us not to remain single and peaceful at any cost.

Father falls upon Mother's piggy bank, where she keeps her secrets hidden away from him. All of the hours of the day, and all the hours of the night, he is the only one who pays in. He is beside himself. Already his sex is almost too heavy to lift. His wife can carry it for a while. In the half sleep of the mornings, he's already fumbling at the furrow in her rear while she is still sleeping, from behind he gropes at her soft hillocks, light, where are you, the heart is already wide awake. The tennis match at his club can wait. It's antiseptic there. First, obedient as children, in go two fingers, into the woman, and then the compact firelighter package is stuffed in to follow. The whole music box where our wishes are stored in the memory of the Supreme Being starts playing music into the ethereal realms. All things will be fulfilled. We have a right to expect it will be so. Take a deep breath! We well know what is best, it's back home on the sideboard. The Man takes hold of his wooden ding-a-ling and batters at the woman's astounded rear entry. She can hear the engine of his loins roaring closer from afar. She's beginning to banish all feeling from within her. But there's still room in the boot! And into the boot goes the heavy genital load, don't worry about the smell. The seats can't be kept clean anyway. Blindly the woman cashes in her security from the Man's spitting dispenser. He is milking her breasts. Let us be at home now. The trees have cast down the leafage of the mountains. The evergreen Man, he does not need to seek the woman's protection, he is mantled in goodwill, not a cloud in the sky. How happy property is to dwell with us. There is no better place for it to occupy than our genitals, which gape wide above it like crags above a torrent. In return this woman gets her life paid out in cash, smack on the table every month, for her everyday oven. Tomorrow once more for the child she will open the door from school into life, this too has been purchased by the Man, and he roasts his hefty sausage in her oven, in its flaky pastry case of hair and skin. But the school bus is stuck fast.

The woman suggests that the child has to eat too. Her husband does not hear. He is leafing abstractedly through his pocket dictionary. The house belongs to him. Already his Word has arrived there and will be taken to heart. He opens wide his wife's genitals to see if his signature there is legible. Angrily he drives his tongue in. It is a knack he acquired out of nowhere one day when he returned from the office. Joyous, the Direktor is a god. And soon he will be in the office joking with his secretary. He has to make a good showing! He tries out ever new positions from which to kick his cart down into his wife's quiet waters and start paddling like a maniac. He doesn't need water wings, he'll never pull one of those plastic things over his red head simply to stay in good health. His wife has been healthy for the longest of times anyway. She writhes beneath him and cries out as a whole herd of seeds plunge stampeding from his well-appointed glans. What's the matter. Only someone who need have no worry about a position or income can clink the ice cubes as loud as this.

This Man, who is now holding his pet tight in the clamp of his thighs, to bite the cheeks and pinch the tits, did after all devise a strategy of his own to cut the firm down to the essential core. Yes, you saw right! And you'll see more still when the gates are thrown open in the morning and the bowed backs of the gleaming herd (having drunk enough) — when they've barely had time to register the sun — disappear again into the darkness and hang up their fate to dry. Right. And every so often one of them is still in his dripping wraps. Who will have mercy on us? Rather let an excessive surplus be earned for the company, than that the superfluous ones, true at least to their wretched names, should earn something for their own homes and gardens. Profit for the foreign multi-national that owns the paper mill. So that he can start up from his sleep bawling, wrap all of us in paper, and gobble us up. The child has his workshop where he is housed and shaped up. At Christmas he performed a solo, standing in front of the manger where there was a dear little child such as himself. This year the snow fell early and it's going to be there a long time too. Sorry about that.

Later one of the woman's neighbours comes to visit, unbidden, uncalled for. The complaints simply pour from her. The abiding weakness of the female sex etc. Which has now awoken and, climbing the stairs, can only break loose out of itself as a complaint. This neighbour is as bothersome as an insect. She shines her light upon the people in the meadows. She confides expressly in the Frau Direktor, and expresses her confidence in the Son of God, who created the people hereabouts out of the earth and transformed their trees into paper, and she hopes He will show favour to her daughter who will soon be finishing her business studies course. Her husband no longer meets her, he meets a twenty-year-old waitress in a station restaurant. The Direktor's wife can think of no more words to say to her visitor. She has no refreshments left to offer her. How lightly she wears her wealth. There she sits, surrounded by furniture and pictures that hadn't a moment's peace till they belonged to her.

Essentially the Man is a big creature of pleasure, a bankable piggy, a citizen singing and gaming. So that his wife's body will be in a state to report for its daily duty, he chooses lingerie for her from a mail order catalogue. And lo, his choice has fallen upon naughty items, so that she can try to be like the models in the photos. But the undies are wasted on her. She leaves them in the drawer, forgotten, and says nothing. No red lace to disturb her peace. But, come to think of it, that's just how he likes it: when his people altogether forget themselves when he uses their love against them. Peacefully they pass like Time in their homes, waiting for him. The child, hungrily stalked by sport. The woman, thirstily compared with photos and films. Families with no dependants and no dependencies simply drive up in their large family car, equipment in the boot: the whips, the birch rods, the fetters, the rubber accessories, all for the big babies whose members are always weeping and wailing and whining for someone bigger than them to come and tame them. Some day their wives will be quiet too and the milk will come. The men even give each other injections, in goes the needle, so they can stay the course longer when they go dropping their coins in the slots of the collecting boxes their wives beseechingly hold out. So that they themselves will be collected again. Calm. Pull themselves together fast. Pull a fast one on their business partners. Women are standing bowed over bowls of salted snacks, laughing, and presently the gentlemen dive onto the sofas, collapse, wag their tails, and then, as fast as they can, flee the ones they have charmed. How deeply the men desire that their shots should go far, far overshoot the mark, the game (what a game)! The women, stretchmarked by their children's sojourn inside them, have to serve themselve up, naked as the day their bundles of joy were born. The weighty wine glasses totter on the trays: their Lords and Masters embrace them from behind, from in front, from anywhere and everywhere, fingers are inserted and withdrawn, mouths suck between thighs. They break their favourite toys. Aha. Now they're resting after their labours of love, the loved ones and the thunderous horsepower that lay with them. The labours of sundry hairdressers have been ruined. There is garbage for charwomen to clear away once again. And then they all go on, and off, in their cars, in the loving arms of their wives. And who, in truth, will be embarrassed before his own car seats? They don't eat chocolate, mind you. The stains, which are all that remains of what we thought the highest of pleasures, tend not to wash out.

The Man can never simply disappear, all of a sudden. He is so settled in his beautiful house. In the evenings, the house is cloaked in the darkness of the forests and mantled in the gloom of the local people: handsomely

turned out! Sympathy would be wasted on the woman.
The pores of her child are still so small. The woman reels
beneath the heavy burden of her happiness. She is under
house arrest, but her sentence may be commuted for
good behaviour. Round and round she goes in the same
old rut; she mustn't deny her circuit judge his rest and
recreation, though. His same old rutting. Barely home
and his whistle's wet again. Company outings generally
end in wetting the whistle, then out it comes, wanting to
be blown, wanting to sound off in the open. Life mostly
consists of things not wanting to stay where they are. So
be it! All change! It all makes for restlessness, unceasing
social intercourse, people go calling on each other but
have to carry themselves with them wherever they go.
Well-ordered servants, there they stand with the
sausages of their sex, banging their cutlery on the table,
wanting a hole to be served up fast, a hole to hide away
in, only to re-emerge greedier than ever, to offer their
hospitable services once again to those who have no need
of them. Not even secretaries care to admit that the
groping that goes on in their blouses is like a denuncia-
tion. They laugh. There are so many of them around
here, too many for them all to get enough of their
improper nourishment.

The Man appears at daybreak. And stands revealed. The
naked truth. He knocks the woman over, slaps her on the
backside, he who has travelled from afar. The tubes are
already rattling on the bathroom shelf, the slip-on cover
is trembling on the toilet, the porcelain is gleaming. You
can hear the silence that has prevailed in the Man's rod
all night. Then he speaks. Nothing can turn him away.
On the level floor stands the woman, weary from her
long and toilsome journey through the night, and now
her socket's due to receive his plug. She has long since
seemed as intimate as a rolling mill: even to his business
associates he brags of her, and in short and powerful
bursts the Direktor's dirty sallies talk their way to the

top. And his subordinates maintain an embarrassed silence. The Man forces himself, we'll be hearing from each other. The Direktor reaches into the pocket of this body, which belongs to him. The loved objects are all there. Nothing missing. The Man is fond of easy talk and the woman is always easy. How could he possibly be expected to contain himself any longer, this silent can opener? Like a plant helplessly seeking the light the moment it's switched off. The child plays very nicely to order. How much better will he perform on his fiddle when one day, like his daddy, he's learnt to work the fiddles of manhood and fatherhood and perform the parts! The long and tedious breast-feeding lies in the child's forgotten past, but he still expects his every wish to be as automatically satisfied. For so long the woman gave of herself to the boy — and what has the trying creature learnt? That you have to try try try again, because heaven is a hill you have to climb, and the climbing has its price.

No, the woman is not mistaken. The boy will long since have put her aside by the time he is a man, and then he will be gone. Now Father drags her into the light, with all his strength, to open her dark tunnel for the express train roaring up. Every day the same. Even landscapes change, be it through sheer boredom, by virtue of the seasons. The woman is passive as a toilet, for the man to do his business in. He shoves her head down into the bathtub and, his hand clawing her hair, threatens that as you make your bed, so you must cry on it, that's love. No, cries the woman. She isn't asking for love. Already the Man is busy with his buttons. Her nightie is hoisted and wrapped around her ears. There is a whimpering in her entrails, like the whimpering of captive animals trying to kick a way out of their cage. The cambric nightdress, bright as a pilot light, is stuffed in the woman's mouth, and the Man appears as Nature made him. His innocent water is passed. Right beside the woman the water splashes from the dark smoke of pubic hair into the tub, past her bowed head. The enamel shines like new. How quickly the Man's tail has grown into a fine upstanding fellow in these friendly surroundings. The woman finds she has to cough while her flanks are being prised open. The can opener is pulled out of the terrifying flannel trousers, and presently a milky fluid appears, in just the time it takes to make a grease stain. His member is hauled out far too early from its drawer into the light. The woman, whose arse has been straddled wide open, a shady lane for the Man to go walking, is left standing. He pulls the helm right round and forces her to look at him. In a rage, he addresses himself to her frontage, forcing her to take hold of his dying willie. There. Already it's starting to twitch again. It wants to dwell within thy hallowed halls! He pushes the woman's hair into his come, what's left of it, let her take a good look, the simpleton. No, they do not rest, the heroes, when their labours are done. The woman is smeared full of sperm. Building her a fine house ensures that a wife will not go missing, and outside stand the paltry terraced houses of the poorest and the unemployed, up for sale, for public auction, or to be torched. And what was once a home is now under the hammer of the local lordsandmasters. What once was work is brutally taken away from these dear hearts. The women, though, can recoup it in small coin. Where else should they go, the women, but to those who splash about in the pool of power? Those who splash out with worthless rubbish that flies from them like foam from teeth? The generators create unnecessary products, the generations create unnecessary problems. This time the Direktor has kept his assets to himself till the right moment. Up front he creams the woman's face with his supersensitive lotion, then she gets an eyeful of his supersensitive parts. To drink in his ichor, truly, is not what she wants, but she must, she must, Love says so, she must groom him and lick him clean and dry him off with her hair. Jesus came first, so to speak, in this. He was wiped dry by a woman. In closing the woman is dealt a slap on the ass, time to close down, a crass lordand-master hand rummages in her slit and probes her orifice, his tongue licks at her nape, her hair hangs down into the tub, he tugs at her clit, and her knees give way and her arse snaps out like a folding chair. And lo, many others are obedient unto his command.

And the boy? What of the boy meanwhile? He's pondering a present he wants bought in return for not having seen any of his plug-and-socket parents' secrets. From every shop he sets eyes on, the child wants another slice of life, cut fresh, only the best, just for him. The child is a devious little rat. The new generation, this. The best is barely good enough. But soon this generation will be passing on as well, moving down the line. How else would we go on?

Father has shot a wad of sperm and now it's up to his wife to clean it up properly. What she doesn't lick up she'll have to wipe up. The Direktor strips off the rest of her clothes and watches her wiping and weaving. One moment her breasts hang forward, the next they bobble about in front of her as she scrubs, making things as new. He pinches her nipples in thumb, index and middle finger, then twists, as if he were trying to screw in a minute light bulb. His raging and weighty entrail slaps out at the window that opens in his trousers and whaps against her thighs from behind. When she bends down she has to spread her legs. Now he can cop hold of her whole fig tree with one hand and set his fingers angrily a-roving. Oh and while she's at it with her legs apart like that she can stand over him and piss in his mouth. What, she can't? Let's see. Up with her knee. There we are (applause, applause!) — the tender lips of her cunt, we'll part them with a soft smacking sound and we men'll be banging our tankards down on the table with a thump. If she still can't pee we'll drag her privates down by the

short and curlies till she bends the knee and splays across
the Herr Direktor's chest. By the hairs he holds the lips
of her cunt parted like a handbag and slushes it across his
face so he can drive his tongue inside, an ox at the
salt-lick, the mountain is on fire. The men bear the load.
Her waters murmur incomprehensibly. And the women
even soak it up with absorbent rags and clean the place
with Ajax.

The woman drinks the cold dregs of coffee from her
dismal cup. As if preparing to flee, she has pulled on her
wispy tights again. There isn't a woman anywhere near
who has it anywhere near as good as she does. Her
lordandmaster's claw rests upon her head, to make her
feel at home in the cage. That evening the Direktor will
be smiling at his weary wife again and setting his sights
on the target. Later his surging banks of foam will crash
against her yet again, his Austrian bank safe against any
crash. The woman reaches into nowhere, where the
food's spoiling, as if she wanted to shake him off the
place of her slumbers. And so they will always be passing
each other by on the broad and perilous highway, the
terrifying mountain railway of marriage. This woman is
envied by the villagers for the fine clothes she wears.
The dirt in her house is vacuumed up by a woman hired
as a cleaner from the catalogue of villagers, who wanted
nothing but to live in brotherhood. The child was born
late, but not so late that he hasn't the time to turn into a
griping adult. The Man shouts out loud with pleasure,
and the woman's voice snuggles against him so that he
will wave his magic wand and produce nice expensive
things for the home. Such as a three piece suite that
can be used at the stations where the two of them go
to rub off their blessed sex. But no one can do magic.
When the Man sobers up he is obliging towards the
woman and good-natured, of course he'll buy her
whatever she wants, he bought everything you see here

in full colour, ladies and gentlemen. So dry your cheeks! There, now.

In the evening, their plates will offer a refuge to food without a home. Fleetingly the dishes are introduced to each other. Then off they go to mingle. In the bodies. What must things be like beneath some people's roofs! Food is of no consequence in this house, all that matters is that there be a lot to eat, so that the stronger of the two can smile and yield in his largesse. Sausage and cheese of an evening, wine and beer and brandy. And milk for the child, to guarantee his growth. That is how the middle class works: safeguarded below and legally protected above. The protection of Nature is done by the ones underneath. So that the whole class doesn't go plummeting into the bottomless depths.

Early in the morning, the Man has already relieved himself. Big are the heaps he dumps, and he's been busy with his pitchfork heaping up more. And how the urine splashes from him! Everywhere under his roof he can be heard. His articulated penis roaring to a standstill in the lay-by of his wife. Where at last he can relieve himself. Lightened of his product, he goes again to the lowly beings who make their own product under his supervision. The paper they have manufactured is an alien thing to them. Nor will it endure for long. The Direktor yells as he bangs and knocks and thrusts. Competitors are banging and knocking at the door, you have to anticipate their next moves, otherwise one or two more of the blessed poor will have to be sacked, or rather: liberated from their toil. Out he goes, the lordandmaster, into Nature, his back bowed with responsibilities, he carries them on his back so he has his hands free. Of his wife, to whom he is a lord, by whom he is restored, he expects that she will be naked beneath the gown of her house when he specially lays back the twenty kilometres from the office to the house. The child will be out of the way. Climbing aboard the school bus the boy fell over his sports gear, what a prick!

The woman awakens quickly from the warm pressure bandage of peace where she has sought refuge. She keeps everything that the boy hastily flung at her as he was leaving. The rest will be dealt with by the house-keeper, who has seen a thing or two in this house and picked it up off the floor, too. When the boy was small, Mother sometimes took him along to the supermarket, where the manager would obligingly escort them personally past the gaggle of waiting housewives. The child would be sitting in the shopping trolley, which was not unlike the womb, and how he liked it there! The thing is, cars built for burning up the track generally have holes in all the wrong places, but still eighteen-year-olds love them more than they love their own families, they can't wait to get away from their parents and parental homes, theirs till death. And then, those magic magnetic security tags on new clothing! Oh, if only people had them too! Then they wouldn't promptly go scotching their prospects when they admire the prospects afforded elsewhere. Sex is going to be safe-guarded against disease as women are safeguarded against the world, so they don't happen to look out of the window without due care and attention and go for a stroll through Life for a change and end up wanting to change their lives. But it's only clothing that is given this security protection in the stores. There's a shrill alarm signal if anyone who shouldn't takes the articles past the check-out, a wanderer out a-roving in the silent realm of the dead and of different brands of coffee. Better to go on foot and poorly clad to our sexual rendezvous. Better to live amidst waste of our own producing. At any rate, we will not have any other vehicle joining our little fleet. And so we keep life forever moving on, following where the road leads, following a friendly face in which we see the terrible reflection of our own.

Only last week the woman bought herself a trouser suit in a boutique. She smiles, as if she had something to hide. Though all she has is the silent realm of her body. Three new pullovers she's purchased she hides away in the cupboard, so that she offers no purchase to mistrust, no occasion for the suspicion that she's using her bloody groove as a ticket to a month of pleasures. The fact is that all she picks from the tree of her Man is that goodly fruit, money. The umbral leafage quilts the trees no longer. The Man checks the cheques she's written, and lo, thousands of trees tossing their topmost branches in the wind are laid low by the axe. The woman's housekeeping money is paid out to her and more! But he doesn't really believe that he actually has to pay for the comfortable rocking chair where he stretches out like a gratified boy, resting his rod. The woman is under the protection of his sir/ surname, his lordandmaster holy-family name, under the shelter of his bank accounts, of which he gives her regular accounts, she has to know what kind of deal she's got, so that as his value appreciates she'll appreciate him the more, and likewise he knows of her garden, ever open, which is ideal for grunting and wallowing. After all, we have to make use of what belongs to us, don't we? Why else would we have it in the first place?

Barely is the woman on her own but she goes out for a walk, escorted by money, securities and depreciation, fine company. Like a shadow she glides through the multitude who make the paper, the sea of paper across which she sails her ship of life, the sea that would bury us all alive, given half a chance! For over there the masses of unemployed fools are lying in wait till someone finally follows their trail. And we? Do we want to fly on, ever on? Smart alecks that we are, first we'll have to climb higher up, to them that shift their arses shall be given.

The woman puts her multi-purpose hand before her eyes. Soon the Man and the child will have to be covered in food again, and what lies ahead tonight? The Man, compact, loaded, fresh from the factory. Waiting to unload. He's been fermenting in his bottle and he wants to uncork the fizz. Tonight, that's right, we almost forgot, how could we, tonight is the legally appointed time for the transaction. And the woman waits with her absorbent cloth to soak up everything the Man has produced during the day. And the rest vanish into the shadows to bury their hopes alive.

The landscape is pretty big, you have to admit. It is a loose fetter upon our fate, which lies shrouded in mist. Two lads out on mopeds promptly come a cropper in the snow. They tumble and go flying. The woman laughs out suddenly. Just for once she would like to go forward decisively. Today her husband showed what he could do in her body, as if there were two of him. Just wait a little. Till evening. When you enter into the circuitry. Now the Man has been drawn off to his office by a steel counter-weight about the size of a telephone. Setting the pebbles flying, he has made it to the armchair behind his desk, from where he controls the fates of others, and to a skiing event on a screen. He loves sport as well. The boy got it from his father. People would simply lie abed patiently and undemanding, if it weren't that the TV screen is full of movement, as are their own feet and hearts at times as well. When the Man speeds along the country road the hairs are flattened on the skin, that's how fast he drives. When he calls for someone, he roars as someone wearing traditional costume would roar. Soon an appearance by the choir will be called for.

On Sunday, as an example of the convivial social life in an army, they go to church. In their coops they have books and memorials of their own enslavement. Nor are the doctor and chemist averse to paying a call on the Pope and the Mother of God. They envy no man his labour. The well-groomed custodians of health, fine fruits of further education, they go to the pub to sit awhile and be jolly. The doctor envies the chemist his shop, the profits of which we wouldn't say no to. The chemist gets people straight from the doctor, with all their weight and blood pressure problems. Lavishly he distributes his preparations amongst the unemployed of the area, so that they will be of good cheer again and will sit outside their houses contentedly twiddling their thumbs. Their wives have provided something to eat, and offer them tasty fare in other ways as well. They won't be deleted from the menu. So the men shall lack for nothing, for men there must be something, the foremen of nothing. Some leave, though a moment ago they seemed at home with us.

Like the woman who works at the bank and is obliged to wear a different dress every day, the Frau Direktor is under certain constraints, and several times a day she draws the freshly cleaned net curtains between herself and the longings of the village women. She would be safer dwelling there than in her own living room. The Direktor talks to the boy. Who jumps and stomps so that he can visit a friend later on. The boy is not entitled to choose his friends to his own satisfaction. The other lads' fathers eat HIS bread! The child is a leader on this earth, steering the others as he steers his toy cars. Mother plays a piano accompaniment to everything, and out there the people rest their weary and discouraged heads on each other's breasts. Their eyes were too big for their bellies. They bought everything they saw. And now the village feasts its eyes when they auction off the houses, which stand all too cheekily on the bare earth. There they stand, the would-be people queueing at the bank, where blessed children in white blouses play with other people's money, to pay in their fates and the fates of their homes, pouring the trickle out of their wage packets into the mighty torrent of interest. The bank manager knows the lie of the land, and he's amazed at the lies people tell so they can keep the houses they built themselves. How they have loved their possessions! And still, so close to home, he has to take everything from them. In his mind's eye the bank manager has fore-suffered all when, no monster he, he looks in at their windows. In this wintry place the poor squabble among themselves. The bolt guns and the hunting rifles crack. Nooses twine about the neck of life. The savings banks are happy as clams, simply messing about with money. For the farming cooperatives it's one long village fête, they don't want to know about the individual, they simply pile high their poisonous cheeses and rotten dairy products on him. And from the very humblest they still take the apple of his eye, and even his nuts as well. Till one day he goes crazy. Flips. Flaps above the nest where he has butchered his dead brood, screaming. How could he have hoped to cope? And in the tabloid papers, for a schilling or so from our pigeon-chested purse, you can read all about the lives of people visited by horror.

What you see from the window is pretty fine: that comely, shapely, strapping lass, Nature. The Man, still the bureaucrat even in his desire, is pursuing a human need, which is not to be confused with the unpleasant need for another human being! There lies the Direktor, like a landscape. But restless. He has smeared on his cheese spread, and what is it he sees in the face of his wife? The human visage of his dictatorship? It is as if the woman had been erased, wiped out, away, wearing her new naughty lingerie. At his request. As if the spatial contours of her life had been redefined. Money plays games with people. From time to time, in his lucid moments, a fit of remorse overcomes the Direktor, and he buries his great big face in the woman's apron. But then it's back to the bathroom to bang her head against the dirty tub again and see if the path that's been cleared goes all the way to her dark doorway. Behind which, there she is, sitting in her own lap, dandled, fondled, spoilt, waiting to have her pages turned to the very last. And how indeed are the unemployed to live in this world if there are not cheap novels to supply examples?

The Direktor, who speaks softly to his staff and has songs sung to him in return, prefers using his tackle on the woman by day, in the bright light. He likes watching his own health increasing. The woman begs him at least to be a little cautious with the child around; the feral creature might leap forth unexpectedly from his corner of the ring at the very last moment. Bang on schedule, the fruit of her womb puts in an appearance, idly looks on for a while as his parents sample the goodies (clutching their plates at the spotless and heavily laden buffet) and vanishes once again, to plague the neighbourhood kids who must grow up without artistic, artificial paradises with his sporting tackle and sporting talk. The boy has ripened in the sun like fruit. Father, depending on your point of view, takes a healthy head-dive into Mother. Words cannot describe it, we want action not words, we have to pay at the entrance to the convenience, and do our duty, which rushes constantly like water.

The little houses have to go to sleep now, but in the big ones there is still life, the current is flowing between the sexes, and, speaking of current, the water flow brings their bodies together. Now we are entirely private. Nor need we be embarrassed in public. And, once the lovers have found each other, they relax and sup at the precious drops that bubble from their gold-labelled bottles. And are at home. Resting in each other once their privates have been excited. They are one. The one and only. Delivered from the dust. And, while all about the poor are dying, the superior classes renew their unspoken rights to each other with every day that comes, and they come too. They have saved up their powers in their piggy banks and in their trousers and hearts. So that they can take a good strong bite from the peach that bloomed so beautiful but a short, short while ago. It is all theirs. Even sleep flatters them, the rapid eye movements of greed cannot be seen behind their closed lids. They must never go unobserved by their loved ones, so every day they sally forth anew, to harvest new finery and fortune, and come staggering home with all they've taken from the staggeringly rich — to be transformed, renewed, daily freshened and restored for the dear soul that they are, have and want to keep. But the weak live together. For they are what we do not want to be. And to crown it all, they imagine they wouldn't want to live anywhere else. They know what they like. Of course, they're not offered the option of liking anything else. And they're woken early, too. Work takes toll of not a single one too many. They are sufficient unto themselves. But we want more! Action! Let there be light — for us! We shall walk forth in the light, and even if it were the light of our own pocket torches, just enough to light the way for two, two members of the flock of the refined: we, we must be the ones! Let there be us!

3

JUICILY, CALMLY, THE MAN inserts the image of his wife into the slit of the viewer. With a shudder the woods reach out for the house, where the video images, a herd of creatures capable of reproduction, are moving across the screen in front of eye witnesses. The women are dragged into the picture by their fetters. Only their daily routine is more merciless. The woman scans the plain as far as the horizon, the vast plain that lies before her every day to be crossed with her husband, then she lies before him on her cross. The Direktor is unbowed by the responsibilities of his job, his sap is rising, he sucks at her tits and slits and bellows for the night to come, for the late show to begin. So too, on mountain slopes, the images grow green, and climbers tread them underfoot in their stout boots.

The unanticipated appearance of the boy is almost as great a tragedy as the weather here. Like a carrier rocket the son, little sunbeam, shoots straight into the room, where the screen is raining its images, pouring its waters. His simple eyes are just in time to register the suffering bodies. Bodies gaping wide like sore and wounded chasms. Bodies visiting, to keep up social intercourse. And the men keeping it up, toiling with the heavy tools of their trade, labouring at their desire. Dying away inside the women. Only their bodies and heads remain outside, and devise new wombs made of glass, to look into. Instantly Father climbs off Mother, letting fly a gusty fart from his gutsy motor, shifting into reverse, and doing a U-turn on the carpet. The boy pretends to have understood nothing. He himself, after all, is a consumer now, scrimmaging and scrummaging: his needs and wishes are like pages in his memory, his taste has been spoilt by the immortal pictures in the sporting goods catalogues, sport is good for the healthy citizen! Everything belongs to him and his dear parents, to whom in turn the child belongs. Mother covers herself hurriedly. As if with hay. The boy has already grasped that evil has a name: Father. But Papa does still buy the baskets of goodies, the sackfuls fat with bulging fun, and binds his son with strings of gold. The child affects not to have noticed the bonds that bind his mother, there on the sofa; instead he reads his parents a list of conflicting wishes. You can drive it on sand, gravel, stone, water, ice and snow! Or a Persian carpet. It has to be bought. So that one can look back from far off in the landscape, back at home. The woman is having fun in her handcuffs, she thrashes her legs, her eyes fixed on the uncertainty that is her child: whatever will become of him? An eaglet gnawing at a sportscar? Beak hacking into the flesh of a human breast? Will he accept defeat in the slalom, which is staked out behind the house and is meant for fun and to accustom humankind to detours? Everything this Man and his manchild wish for is dangerous in one way or another. With her teeth Mother tries to pull a blanket over her bare nipples, into which Father has just sunk his teeth. Abruptly the images on the screen are lulled asleep. The child is there. The child wants a motorized sleigh, but in these parts motorized sleighs are officially banned. Customers are entitled to have their demands met; the woman has to look the part.

The Direktor expects to be able to phone home at any time at all, including office hours, to check that he is being thought of. He is as inevitable as death. Always to be at the ready. To tear her heart out. To lay her heart on her tongue like the host, and to show that the rest of her body is in readiness for the Lord, as he expects of his wife. To this end he keeps the bridle on his bride. He keeps her under his watchful eye. He sees everything, he has a right to examine whatever he wishes. For his prick it bloometh in its prickly bed, and on his lips the kisses bud and blow. But first he has to take a good look at everything, to work up an appetite. For you eat with your eyes too. And nothing remains concealed, excepting heaven unto the eyes of the dead, who placed their hope in it at the last. Which is why the Man wants to make a heaven on earth for his wife, and she sometimes makes the food. You can get away with requesting it three times a week, her famous Linz gateau. And as for the famous Linz dictator, the Man can voice his regard for him in the back room at the pub, where those assembled take solace in History's merciful ability to repeat itself, and look into a glass, darkly, to see what the government has in store for the country.

The Direktor is so vast that you couldn't get around him in a day. He is open to anything, especially the rain and snow that come from up above. There is no one above him, except the parent company, that is, but there is no protection against it. When it's a matter of his wife's sharp edge, though, it's no problem opening up the tap and letting it spurt out. The woman twitches like a fish. Her hands being bound. While the Man tickles and prickles her a little with pins. He pricks an ear at the store of feelings he's hoarded deep within. Words fall from the video screen like leaves, they fall to the floor, floored by this one-man win in the human race. At a loss, the woman casts a protective glance at a dying plant on the window sill. Now the Man is saying something. Words as meaty as steak. He doesn't mince them. As his blood and juices gather, he talks incessantly of what he will do and what he won't be able to help doing, and he uses his savage claws and tame teeth to gain access to his objective, to add mustard to his sausage. His wife's sex is a wood from which an angry echo returns to him.

Recently he forebade his wife Gerti to wash. For her smell too belongs to him entirely. He ransacks his little woodland, heaves the weighty heel of his loaf into her bread bin, a nuisance that she is often so swollen, damn it! Ever since his guts failed him and he stopped the small-ad search for strangers desirous of swopping wives, he's preferred it to be the gusts of his own desire that search out his wife. Lifting her skirts. He wants her trailing a banner of sweat, piss and shit scents. And he checks that the stream is flowing in its own bed where it belongs. A living heap of garbage. Where worms and rats go burrowing. With a bellow he takes the plunge, he gets a move on, quickly reaching the far end where his home is and he'll be cosy again and now and then he'll toss one back or simply watch the fishes jump. He reads the papers. He drags the woman from the swamp of her cushion and cracks her open. And there on the sofa yet again he has his nice little toy complete with tits to play with, trembling at what his veins have done with his member.

He likes to have this woman, the best-dressed woman in the village, going about the house in her own dirt. Angrily he hits her about the head. In their transubstantiation he has had her body rebuilt to his specifications. It is a vessel designed for copious giving. He too is replenished nightly, his self-service store, his toy grocer's where it's perfectly okay to set a little something aside. The front door key confers the right to today's special, clit served any way you want it, or you can slam the toilet door; the Roman Catholic homeland is flexible, but it allows people to go to pregnancy counselling or the altar. The house has to send out SOS signals while the woman is being utilized. Later a choice bottle of wine will be uncorked and the screen will show other bottles being uncorked, pop! and the choice bodies will examine each other's genitals, rattle at the handle and cast their seed on stony ground. How greedy we are to watch them. But others are watching us. Crunching salted snacks, nibbling the gentlemen's sausages or the ladies' titbits.

The boy will perhaps stay at the neighbours' tomorrow.

They have an exactly identical house, only less of it. The Man wants to drive his savage cart into the woman's dirt. Who practises breath control and has to dive to one side to escape his prick as it crashes into the undergrowth of her panties. His body has had an overpowering effect on all kinds of people, thanks to music and song, they have been packaged up in portions and deep-frozen for later when they will be needed on the job market or to sing in the choir of market forces. The moon is shining, oh look, the stars are shining too, and the Man's machine comes crashing and roaring home from afar, ploughs up the furrow she has cleared with her teeth, sets the cut grass flying like spray, and pumps the woman full to the brim.

4

THE WOMAN, HER BODY flailing awkwardly, strikes out into the wind. She has been made flesh and has dwelt among us. Her off-sales service has ministered to the hungry in every way: she has been worn out by the Man and by the child, sweetest of bridles and reins. Caught in the net, she tries to catch her breath for once. Throwing on her dressing-gown, she sets out trudging down the snowed-up path in her slippers.

First, in case of emergency, she has to put the cups and kitchen utensils away in the cupboards. Under the flowing water she scrubs the traces of her family off the china. And so the woman preserves herself in the very accessories that she is made of. She arranges everything, even her own clothing, according to size. Ashamed, she laughs at the fact. But it's no joke. Orderly arrangement is added to the blessings she already enjoys. She herself is left with nothing. Of the bloody bird feathers on the path there is little to be seen now, for even animals must eat. A sooty layer coats the snow, it took just a few hours.

In his office, the Man reaches contentedly under the lampshade of his waistband and lets a little air in. He talks of his wife, of her figure, without troubling to indicate that it's his turn to speak. Be quiet, now his works are speaking for him, there is a choir of many voices for that specific purpose. No, he is not afraid of the future. His purse is full, and the more he spends, the more he gets!

The woman senses the snow gradually invading time and space. Springtime is still a long way off. Not even today can Nature manage to look freshly painted. The trees are grimed with muck. A dog hobbles past her in a hurry. Women come along the path, looking as if they'd been stored in cardboard boxes for years. As if they had awoken in a fine house, the women inspect this other odd one out, who keeps herself to herself. The factory provides many of their husbands with work, what else? Unconscious before their time, they'd rather spend their time wih a bottle of wine than their family. The woman glides past them into the gloom, she hasn't even put on shoes to go out in the snow! Meanwhile the child is out and about somewhere, romping with more of the same. He refused the food she'd cooked, refused with words that tore great gaping gashes in his mother, and went off with a *wurst* sandwich instead. For much of the morning, Mother had been straining carrots through a sieve, for the boy's eyes. She cooked the lad's food herself. And then, a bent stalk of humanity, she gobbled up the boy's helping herself, standing by the bin. When all's said and done, she did produce the child from out of her own self. Her sense of humour has not grown, though. From the fence by the stream hang icicles, the capital is not far away as the car drives. It is a broad valley, and not many are employed in it. The rest, since everybody has to be somewhere, are at their onerous places of employment: they go to work at the paper mill every day, while others commute even further afield, much further! Up there on the mountain is where I love to be, with my flock. The woman's mouth freezes as tiny as a marble. She clings to the iced-up wood of the railing. The stream is bridged from both banks, the ice is slapping its back, Creation is groaning under the fetters of natural law. There's a faint gurgling sound. Just as the thaw will melt all the barriers in this good life we all lead, levelling us so that there are no distinctions any more, so too Death may be the *reductio ad absurdum* of this woman's world. But let's not be personal. The wheels of a small car crunch and bite through the tightly-packed snow. Wherever it comes from, it's more at home there than its owner is. What would the commuter be without it? A dung heap.

Because when he's pitchforked into a carriageful of humanity he's simply dirt, that's how his parliamentary representatives see it. It's a question of crowds, of masses: they're what prevent our economy from collapsing, bunched inside our factories, propping them up from within. And as for the unemployed! A shadowy army of nothings, who do not need to be feared because all of them vote for Christian Social Democrats notwithstanding. Herr Direktor is flesh and blood and eats his full share thereof as well because ladies in aprons serve it to him.

You are advised not to drive in this weather if you can avoid it. On the other hand, you are expected to be at your place of work on time. To this tune, the trucks are out, gritting the streets, leaving their wares. All the woman has to offer is herself. Oh, and one more thing: don't call out the emergency services unless it's absolutely essential! The poor creatures. You wouldn't like it either.

The children howl down the well-ironed snow into the valley in their plastic birthday shells which stick to their skin or fly past their ears. Sullenly the older ones turn away, their chair-lift tickets dangling at their padded rotundities. Speed is not magic. They roar like railway stations. The woman is frightened of them. Alarmed, she cowers in the cornices of snow left by the snow plough. Grinding and crunching, cars loaded with families, whole cargoes of miserable beatings, trundle past her. On the roof racks the skis are at full stretch to restrain the hatred of the passengers. The skiing tackle stares down belligerently like machine guns. They plough through the many other containers of humanity because they merit a better place. So thinks everyone. And shows it by making endearingly filthy gestures out of the window.

Sport! The fortress of the common man! From which he
can do his shooting.

Believe me, everybody, but everybody, can afford to
break a foot or both arms! Still, you can't help feeling
that these people are dependants, up the hill they go and
then come gliding down it and even feel good doing it.
But dependent on what? On their own images. And, as if
they themselves were no more than midwives of reality,
the images are screened anew every day, but bigger,
better, faster. And thus, kicked down from the television
watershed, they tumble to the other side, where the
ordinary people mill on the hill of idiots. Ouch. In
discussions they never get a word in edgeways. And if
they do they are instantly interrupted by someone who
ranks as an expert, who doesn't share their worries
about rank. And the Supreme Being, who has studied the
rankings, is deaf to their whining for a home of their
own, which they say they need so that they won't have to
sally forth — they can sully sport, that silly Aunt Sally of
an Olympian idea, on their very own doorsteps.

The woman slips and slides at every step she takes. In the
car windows laughing faces appear, soundless. The
driver comes within a whisker of death. The snow falls
amply on one and all. But they all ski differently, just as
no two human beings are alike. Some are better than
others, and others want to be best of all. Where is the lift
slope for every degree of difficulty so that there will
quickly be more of us? What was slack and limp in its
house just now is firmed up when it emerges into the air.
But it looks all the smaller. Thanks to the sturdy Alps!

The woman emerges from the cover of her circumstances. Out of humour, she hugs her dressing-gown
tightly to herself. Flails her arms about. Some of the
children she hears yelling from afar have been torn from
their weekly dance and rhythm class. These children

were bred as this woman's hobby. After all, we've got
enough room and love for the child to set him clapping
rhythmically. That will help him to nod his head in time
at school or stand up when it's time for prayers. There
her son is, in the midst of them, demonstrating with
every step he takes that he is a grubby finger above them
all, poised to smudge them. He has to take first bite of
every *wurst* sandwich. For every child has a father. And
every father has to earn money. On his junior skis, the
boy terrorizes the little kids on their toboggans. He is the
latest edition of a bright star that has the gall to appear
every day, always wearing different clothes. None of the
others rebel. Though his back has to put up with a lot of
covert and wasted gestures. Already he sees himself as a
phrase expressed by his father. The woman isn't wrong,
vaguely she raises a hand to wave at her distant son,
whom she has recognized by his voice. He barks the
other kids to attention, the way he wants them, and his
words cut them down to dirty heaps as does winter the
landscape.

The woman writes characters in the air with her hand.
She does not have to earn her living, she is kept by her
husband. When he returns home at the end of the day he
has earned the right to set his signature to life. That child
was no accident. The boy is his! Now he no longer sees
death ahead.

With pent-up love she seeks out her son in the troupe of
children. He bawls and bawls and still he doesn't tire.
Was he like that when he crept from her ground floor,
the womb of Mother Earth? Or, as his heavenly father
would put it, was he first led astray, were the arts of life
at work on him, carving him into something he was not,
that no boy at this age ever was or ever shall be? The
child claims rights of those who think differently, rights
as inclusive as the treaties signed by nations. He parrots
his father's expressions: you have to grow a little every

day! Great! An erection! Men are always a little ahead of themselves so that they can look at themselves whenever they want. And the child, made of a being that has long since, like clinker, fallen down behind him (the bell foundry of his mother), will presently, in a year or so, squirt high as heaven where little ones are welcomed in to have a snack.

The boy goes racing through the midst of comrades and cameras as if through open and welcoming doors.

The cold has stolen into the woman's feet. The soles of her slippers are not worth mentioning, but she herself doesn't say much anyway. The soles barely protect her mortal soul from the ice of the world. She stomps on. Better look out. Slide, don't let the others shove you. But people are forever shoving. What else should it mean when the golden-headed sexes, after a fashion, open up in front of the furniture, sole intimates and witnesses of their talents? What if they were to be slung derisively off the summits of their wishes? The woman is holding onto the railing and making good headway. Foodstuffs are being lugged homeward all around, for meals are the main thing in family life. Rolled oats spray from the women's mouths, I'd say they were worried what the expensive ingredients might get up to in the pan. And the men are there, at their plates, filled with a sense of event. The unemployed, who have deviated from the kind of life intended by God and blessed in the sacrament of matrimony, can just about afford to live, but the good life isn't on the cards: no adventure playground, no casino, no cinema watching a lovely film, no café with a lovely woman. The only thing that comes free is the use of their own families. The boundary lines are drawn by sex. Which Nature surely can't have planned, at least not like this. Nature shares the good life with us so that we can eat of her produce and be eaten in turn by the owners of factories and banks. Interest would have the shirt off

our back. But no one can say what water does. It's plain
to see what is done to the water, though, with the
cellulose plant pumping its waste into the stream, which
is in no hurry to get anywhere. Let it pump its poison
somewhere else, where people like their streams to
supply dead fish to eat. The women examine the shopping
bags which they used to get rid of the dole money.
Consumers are well advised in the stores, where special
offers are announced over the public address. Special
offers are what they themselves were, once! And their
men were chosen according to their means. But now
they are treated as the meanest of creatures at the labour
exchange. Sitting at the kitchen table, drinking beer and
playing cards, a dog's life. But not even a dog would be so
patient, kept on its lead outside the wonderful stores
filled with fine wares that mock us.

Nothing is ever lost. The state is at work with what we
don't see. Where does our money go, once we have
finally got rid of it? We burn to be done with it, the notes
are hot in our hands, the coins melt in our fists. Yes, we
must part. Time shall stand still on payday so that we can
stop and take a good look at our stinking and steaming
heap of money, still warm from our labours, before we
transfer it to our accounts. One day we'll be in clover.
What we'd like best of all would be to lie back and rest
amid our hot golden nuggets of dung. But love, ever
restless, is already looking around to see where there's
something better than what we've already got. The
people who live where skiing originated, people who
once grew here like grass (the world's most famous
skiing museum is at Mürzzuschlag, Styria!) are familiar
with it only by sight. They are stooped so far forward
over the cold ground that they cannot find the trail.
Continually others are passing them, to do their business
in the woods.

Like a horse the woman tugs at her reins. Embarrassed,

in their Sunday best, the strangers brought together by
an ad in the personal column used to sit on her sofa,
mostly two by two. Dejected, the woman giggled, toying
with the glasses on the coasters, and the men, the
members of the club, were out coasting, their members
wanting new toys. Unbuttoned, unbraced. Wanting to
change to a new feed bag once every so often. Standing
poised at the living room table, slinging the women's legs
to left and right about their shoulders. When you're on
your travels it's nice to leave your old familiar ways
behind; and then, when you return home, how com-
forting it is to go back to those old ways. At home the bed
is a four-square thing on solid ground. The women, who
go to the hairdresser every week, are properly put
through their paces, because that's what they thrive on.
Well-upholstered bodies, well-upholstered suites, an
orgy of fleshy padding, as if we'd won an unlimited
supply of experience in a lottery. Intimate lingerie is sold,
so that experience — the kind of experience we women
hopefully and vainly long for — will look different when
it comes to call and we are asleep and turn over and store
it up.

By the pricking of his flesh, and the liberties taken by the
press, the Direktor is unceasingly goaded onward. He
takes liberties himself, e.g. he pees on his wife as dogs do.
Having first made a little mountain of her person and
clothes so that it's downhill all the way. The scale of
desire is open-ended, what Richter would presume to
judge? The Man uses and dirties the woman as if she
were the paper he manufactures. He is responsible for
the well-being or otherwise of this household, greedily
he yanks his tail out of the bag before he has even shut
the door and stuffs it, still warm from the butcher's, into
the woman's mouth, setting her teeth on edge. Even if
they have company for dinner, bearing their light into
his darkest recesses, he still manages to whisper sweet
nothings about her genitals in his wife's ear. Uncouthly

his mitt gropes her under the table, burrowing into her furrow, taking her fear, which strains at the lead, for a walk in front of his business associates. The woman has to be kept on a short leash so that she knows what's what. She has to be ever mindful of the pungent solution he could steep her in. Man and wife must cleave together, so he laughs and reaches into her cleavage before their guests. Which one among you has no need of paper? A satisfied customer is king. And which of you has no sense of humour?

The woman goes on. For a while a big strange dog joins her, hoping to be able to bite her foot, since she isn't wearing proper shoes. The Alpine Association has issued its warning: there's death in the mountains. The woman kicks the dog. She doesn't want anyone or anything expecting anything of her. The lights will soon be switched on in the houses, and every hearth will then be a place of truth and warmth, and the hammering and chiselling will be starting up inside the women.

The valley is peopled with the wishes of part-time farmers. The children of God. Not of the personnel manager. The valley shoves up closer, like an excavator digging up the woman's footsteps. She walks by the immortal souls of the unemployed, whose number increaseth year by year as the Pope commanded. Youngsters flee their fathers and are chased by curses sharp as axes through the empty sheds and barns. The factory kisses the good earth from which it has taken the all too acquisitive people. We have to find ways of rationalizing our approach to the federal forests and federal funds. Paper is always needed. Now look: without a map, we would be headed straight for the abyss. Somewhat embarrassed, the woman thrusts her hands in the pockets of her dressing-gown. Her husband does take an interest in the unemployed, believe me:

even if they are not kept busy, the thought of them keeps him busy, he never stops, never a moment's rest.

In the mountain stream there are no chemicals learning to swim at this upper reach, just the occasional human faeces. The stream tosses restlessly in its bed beside the woman. The slopes are steeper now. Over there, round the bend, the sundered landscape is growing back together again. The wind is growing colder. The woman doubles over. Her husband has already kick-started her twice today. Then at last his battery seemed to be flat. So off he drove to the factory, taking the hurdles on the way in massive voracious leaps, leaving them under his tyres. The ground crunches underfoot, a grinding sound, but it's not the grinding of teeth, they're hidden underneath. At this height there's little but rocks and mud off the scree. The woman has long since lost all feeling in her feet. This path can't be leading anywhere but a small sawmill at best, the grinding of teeth has ceased there too, it's silent most of the time, how can you say anything anyway without your teeth in. We are on our own. The occasional crofts and cottages by the wayside are equal, they have similarities. Old smoke rises from the rooftops. The occupants are drying out their floods of tears by the stove. Garbage is heaped by the outside toilets. Battered enamel buckets that have served for fifty weary years or more. Stacks of wood. Old crates. Rabbit hutches from which run rivers of blood. If Man can kill, so too can the wolf and the fox, his great role models. Slyly they slink by the chicken runs. Nighttime visitors. Domestic pets get rabies from them and pass it on to Man, their lordandmaster. Eat and be eaten. Take a good hard look. Like what you see?

There she is, tiny when seen from our vantage point: the woman, at the end of the path, passing by, like time. Already the sun is very low. Clumsily it is sinking towards the crags. The child's heart is beating elsewhere.

For sport. This Son of Man, this woman's child, is a coward, to tell the truth. Away onto the flat he steers his toboggan and he's out of earshot. Now, at the latest, the woman ought to turn back. Up ahead there is only some character on a cross, magnificently out-suffering all who have ever suffered since. Given this beautiful view it's hard to decide if we should have this moment last forever, and forgo the rest of the time that we're entitled to. Photographs often record this dilemma; but afterwards we're glad we're still alive and can look at the photos. It's not as if we could send in that remainder of time and receive a free gift in return. Still, we always want things to be beginning and never ending. Out into Nature go the people, hoping to return with an impression which their weary feet have made on the earth. Even the children want only to exist. As quickly as possible. On the slope with the ski lift. The moment they've tumbled out of the car. And we take a deep and innocent breath.

This woman's child still can't see further than the end of his nose. His parents have to do that, they even have to clean the nose, and they offer prayers unto heaven that their offspring will beat everyone else's by a nose. Wetly, he sometimes offers his mother his mouth, his face half free of its halter, the horse collar of the violin already off. And as for his father. In the hotel bars of the county town he talks of his wife's body as he might talk of the founding of an association sponsored by his factory, though soon he'll be relegated to a lower division. The words that come from Father's lips have a pungent odour. You wouldn't find them in a book. To leave a living human being dog-eared and tattered like that and not even read her! Centuries will come and centuries will go and still this Man will bounce back. Jesus: you can't keep a good man down.

This morning the woman was in a waking dream, a

waiting dream, at the house, aimless, waiting for her
husband, waiting on her husband, orange juice or
grapefruit juice? So that he would catch her scent. Lick
her off. Angrily, on the wing, he points at the jam. For it
is written that she shall wait for him till evening when he
cometh to bed down in her lap. Every day he uses his
appliance as he has done for many a year. And what an
impressive score he's run up. Men like scoring, one way
or another. They're born with a target in their breast,
their fathers send them over the hills and far away, just
to shoot at other men's targets.

The ice is thick on the ground. The grit lies scattered
carelessly as if someone had emptied his pockets. The
municipal authorities grit the roads so that vehicles don't
break their tyres. The pavements for people aren't
gritted. The idleness of the unemployed is a burden on
the budget, but as they idle by they do not burden the
snow. Their fate is in the hands of someone who already
has his hands full with a wine glass and plateful from the
ample buffet of cold cuts. The politicians have to wear
their big and bursting hearts on their tongues. The
woman gets a firm footing on the verge. Here, the law of
the catalytic converter rules: unless money is thrown
at it, the environment won't react to us ambitious
wanderers. And even the wood would have to die. Open
the window and let feeling in! Then Woman will show
that disease afflicts the Man's world.

Flailing helplessly, Gerti stands on the ice. Offering
herself. Her dressing-gown flapping about her. She
claws at thin air. Crows caw. Her limbs fling forward as
if she had sown a whirlwind and couldn't grasp the
soughing and blowing on Mother's Day or the slurping
of the Man at her trough when he appears below the
table to lick the cream from her bowl. Woman is forever
earthbound, they compare her with the earth, so she will
open up and receive the Man's member. Perhaps lie

down in the snow for a while? You wouldn't believe how many pairs of shoes this woman has at home! And who is it that's always egging her on to buy more clothes? For the Direktor, people count simply because they're people and can be used or else can be made into consumers who use things. That is how the unemployed of the area are addressed, who are in line to be eaten up by the factory when all they want is something to eat themselves. For the Direktor, they count doubly if they can sing for their supper. Or play the accordion or fool. Time passes, but we want it to say something to us. Not a moment of peace and quiet. The stereo drones eternal: listen, if patience and not the violin is what you play, what you have, oh sainted ones! The room is uplifted, a ray of light falls upon us, the beatitudes of sport and leisure cost the earth, and on the operating tables we re-enter the peaceable kingdom, resurrected, whole again.

5

THE SUPERMARKETS ARE bursting with captivating goods, people are their captives. On Saturday the Man is supposed to be a partner, helping take in the catch in the nets. The fishermen sing. It is a simple tune and by now the Man has managed to learn it. Without saying a word he stands among the women who are counting their loose change and fighting starvation. How are two human beings supposed to become one if humankind cannot even join hands in a chain for peace? The woman is accompanied, the packages and bags are carried, no fuss, no noise. The Direktor is expensively showy in public, taking up the space that is other people's, checking to see what they're buying, though that is really a matter for his housekeeper. He is a god, scurrying to and fro among his creatures, who are less than children and collapse beneath temptations vaster than the ocean. He looks in other people's baskets and down cleavages, where undesirable colds are revealed and hot desires are concealed by neck-scarves. The houses tend to be cold and damp, so close to the stream. His wife's hand is rummaging among dead cellophane-wrapped creatures in the freezer, and when he looks at her, the paltriness of her meat, her fine clothes, he is beset by terrible impatience to let her partake of his own ample meat, his dong, his wonderful shlong. He wants to see it stir at the feeble touch of her fingers like a creature roused by the sun. He wants to see that little animal of his awake at the touch of her varnished talons and bed down again to sleep inside the woman. She'd better make an effort, in her silk blouse, so that he doesn't always have to do all the troublesome work himself, manhandling her breasts out and placing them on the plate of his hands. Why can't she serve herself up, be a little obliging, so he doesn't have to waste half an hour picking the fruit from the tree first. In vain. He pauses before the check-out to survey the gaping emptiness of his property, before which the goods are sitting up and begging, good boy. A number of supermarket employees are dancing attendance on him, who has taken their children away, some for his factory, others because they are having to move or become alcoholics. He is their lordandmaster and even lords it over time.

The shopping bags have done what was required of them, they rustle and bustle through the hall, helped on their way by a kick from the Direktor. From time to time he tramples on the food in a temper, so that it squirts in the air. Then he tosses the woman in amongst the other goods to complete the picture, and she is allowed to breathe his air and lick his penis and anus. With a practised hand he catches her tits as they fall from her dress, they are already sagging and wilting but he gathers them into bunches like balloons with a firm grip. He seizes the woman by the nape and bends over her as if he meant to pick her up and stuff her in a sack. The furniture is glimpsed fleetingly as if it were on a flying visit. Clothes are scattered. You wouldn't say these two were exactly attached to each other, but in a moment they are well and truly attached to each other; funny, that. This particular patch has been used for grazing for years. The Direktor yanks out his product, which isn't paper, it's altogether harder, these are hard times after all. People like showing what they have hidden about them to each other as a sign that they have nothing to hide, that everything they say to their inexhaustibly flowing partners is true. They send out their members, the only messengers that always return to them. You can't say the same of money, for instance. Though it is loved more dearly than the hooves and horns of the loved one, already gnawed at by dogs. The products are produced, to the accompaniment of shrieking and thrashing, the tiny body factories grind and crunch, and the modest property, burdened down only by the happiness babbling forth from the lonely TV set, pours into a lonely pool of sleep where one can dream of bigger commodities and more expensive products. And humanity flourishes on the bank.

The woman lies wide open, open wide, on the floor, slippy slithery eatables slopped upon her. Stock still. Only her husband is permitted to deal in her stocks and bonds. An honest broker. He falls from himself into the furnished emptiness of the room. Only his own body comes anywhere near doing justice to him. At sports, if required, he can hear himself sound and echo. The woman has to crook and angle her legs like a frog so that her husband, the examining magistrate, can look into the matter closely. A court of no appeal. She is flooded and shat full him, she has to get up and the last of her clothes fall on the floor and she fetches a sponge to clean the Man, that irreconcilable enemy of her sex, of himself and the slime that she has caused him to emit. He sticks his right forefinger up her arsehole and, tits dangling, she kneels above him and scrubs. Hair in her eyes and mouth. Perspiration on her brow. Another person's saliva at the base of her throat. The pale killer whale there before her till the friendly light dies, night comes, and the animal can begin to lash her with his tail again.

They are usually silent as they return from the supermarket. Some of them, trying out their horsepower, hurry on by, and are unforgivingly preserved in memory. The milk churns by the wayside, the atoms breathing terribly in and out of them, stand waiting for collection. The farming co-operatives are at each other's throats, all of them competing; they cannot for very long bear the scrutiny of even the smallest holder, who cannot supply much milk and who cannot even be allowed to bleed dry. The woman is cloaked in the darkness of silence. But then she laughs, laughs till it seems she will never stop, to humiliate her husband. The pedantic patriarch. Such notions, keeping such a close eye on the girl at the check-out. Like so many of the wives of the unemployed, she mustn't make even the slightest mistake. The Direktor steals up beside her, she has to enter all the items again to make sure there isn't a single one too many. It's almost the same as in his factory. Except that the people here are smaller and wear women's clothing, from out of which they look about, finding that the family fits tightly and pinches. The Direktor has been known to pinch too. They fold in their wings, and from their bodies the children shoot forth, and the fathers zap their flashing lightning into the kiddies' newly-opened eyes. Disorganized flocks of women shoppers, intent on their shopping, shove past the ones who are enchanted by the goods, trying to make it to the grave as soon as they can. Their heads rise sheer as cliffs at the special offers. There are no freebies for this lot, quite the contrary, they are relieved of a part of their earnings from the paper mill. Horrified they stare at the boss, whom they hadn't expected to see here and of whom, to be plain, they were hardly thinking at all. Often we open our doors only to be confronted with people we hadn't been expecting at all, and then we're supposed to feed them. Salted sticks and potato snacks are all we can come up with to overshadow them.

Gorges of shelving recede to the distant horizon. The bunch of people disperse. Already the last of their wishes, like the straps of sweaty vests, are slipping from their weary morning shoulders. Sisters, mothers, daughters. And the holy Direktorial couple, in perpetual repetition, are on their way back to the penal colony of sex, where they can whine for redemption to their heart's content. All that they receive in their cell, through the flaps and holes, is gruesome gruel, luke-warm, poured over their outstretched hands. Sex, like Nature, has its following. Who enjoy its products. And wear frilly lace for the purpose and the products of the

cosmetics industry. Yes, and perhaps sex is the nature of
humanity. I mean, it is in humanity's nature to chase
after sex, until taken whole the one and the other are of
equal importance. An analogy may convince you: you are
what you eat. Till work pulps the human creature into a
grubby heap. A melted snowman. Till, marked with the
weals of his origins, he no longer even has a hole to
retreat into. How long it takes, till humanity has finally
been questioned and learns the truth about itself . . .
While we're waiting, why not listen to me. These
unworthy creatures are important and hospitable for
just a single day, the day they marry. Only one year later
they are made liable for the furniture and car. The whole
family is liable for the crimes of one member if he can't
keep up the payments. They even buy beds on the never-
never, the beds they frolic in! Smile into the faces of
strangers who lead them to their mangers. So that a stalk
or so of hay wisps in the breath of sleep.

Before they move on. But we, we have to get up at an
ungodly hour every day. Alone and in a far-off place, we
merely gaze down our narrow road, where the sweet-
hearts we couple with are now the objects of other
desires, to be used by others. They say a fire burns
within women. But it's only dying embers. The shadow
of afternoon falls on them in the morning when they
creep from the gullet of attic bedrooms, where they have
to look after a bawling child, into the maw of the mill. Go
home, if you're tired! No one envies you. No one finds
your beauty disarming any more. He hasn't for a long
time. Rather, he strides out briskly, leaving you, and
starts his car, where the dew lies fresh and glinting in the
first bright highlights of sunshine. Quite unlike your
matt and dull hair from which the glinting highlights
have gone forever.

The factory. My, how it deals with the unskilled folk who
are pumped into it from inexhaustible sources. And how

loud it is, inexhaustibly drowning the din of the stereos! A whole houseful of humanity. A factory built on the Direktor's lot. His plot. Who did it? they wonder, fetching a refreshing Coke from the dispenser. A tent of light and living creatures, where paper is manufactured. Rival firms are putting the competitive screws on, and if anyone ends up getting screwed it'll be the employees at the mill. The company that owns the factory in the adjoining federal province has far more clout and is right on a major traffic artery, the bleeders. Wood is pulped and the pulp is processed at the mill by people who've been pulped, at least that's what I've been told, and I'm glad that I, being free, can go into the silent woods in the heat of the day and spew my echo out. The armies of the irresponsible, people like me, who read their papers on the toilet, see to it that the trees disappear from the woods so that they can take the trees' places and unwrap their food from paper wrappings. Then at night people drink and worry. And when there's a dispute, the bloated and blinded multitude plunges into the depths of night.

The factory has gone to the wood. But it has long since been pining for somewhere else, somewhere that production costs are lower. The divine hoardings that line the arterial roads set the hordes dreaming and steaming off on their toy train sets. But the points all point to nowhere. And even the Herr Direktor is in the hands of the powers that be. Gobbling public money. Opaque are the policies of the owners, whom no one knows. At five in the morning people fall asleep at traffic lights on their hundred-kilometre drive to the factory. At the very last crossroads, at the very last holy red light that toys with them, they fail and are killed, failing to slam on the brakes, failing to break off their dreams of the last grand slam Saturday night. Those TV caresses, which for years have nourished their pawing and panting, they'll never see again.

And so they all cause their women to sound forth once more, that they might not hear the last trumpet at least till next pay day. The trumpet call of rumour never falls silent in this place. Those who have been dropped by the banks sit chirruping in the furrows, eating their last crumbs of bread. Behind them a wife wanting her house-keeping money and new books and exercise books for the children. All of them are dependent on the Direktor. That big kid with the mildest of tempers. Though his temper can snap round with a crash, like a sail, and then we're all in the same boat. And promptly fall out on the vast, wild side. The side we flung ourselves across to at the very last moment. Because we don't know how to strike up our thousand-voiced siren song to better effect. Even in our anger we are forgotten. But our running sore is hurting. And we run wild.

6

THE WOMAN GROPES HER way along a fence by an old volunteer fire brigade station, failing in her confused state to find the emergency exit from her memories. There she goes, not even on a lead. The dirty washing-up waiting to be done is clean gone from her mind. Already she has ceased to hear the familiar jingling of the bells on her bridle. Speechless, she licks up like a flame, like sparks. She's left them both behind, her practical-minded husband who is a great sport and is still growing, regardless of the flames shooting from his genitals, and her child, all gut and screech like his violin playing. Let them drone and howl together. Ahead of her is only the cold tempestuous wind off the mountain. The terrain is threaded by a few paths leading into the woods. Dusk. In their cells, the housewives bleed from the brain, from the sex they all belong to. What they have bred they must now tend and rear and keep alive and cradle, in arms already laden down with hopes.

The woman moves towards the icy channel in the cleft of the valley. Awkwardly she wanders across the frozen clods. Now and then animals are revealed through an open stable door, then there is nothing. The rear quarters of the animals, pulsing craters of mud, are turned to face her. The farmer isn't exactly in a hurry to clean the shit off their hind parts. In the large livestock sheds in wealthy regions, the animals are given an electric shock through the yoke about the head if they crap at the wrong time: cattle training. Beside the cottages, wood is stacked, wretchedly snuggling up to the wall. The least you might say of Man and Beast, their common denominator as it were, is that both are tucked fast in their beggarly beds by the snow. Sparse plant life, tough leafage, is still straining for the light. Iced-over twigs play with the water. To be stranded here of all

places, on this ice-tight bank where even echoes founder!
Nature presupposes sheer scale: anything of a smaller
size could never excite us or entice us, tempt us to buy a
dirndl dress or a hunting outfit. Just like cars approaching
a distant country, so we too, like stars, are nearing this
unceasing landscape. We simply can't stay at home.
Someone's put a country inn there, just for us, to put an
end to our rambling. And Nature is put where it belongs,
with a preserve for domesticated deer or a path through
the woods with every tree labelled for our instruction. In
no time, we know all there is to know about it. There are
no mountainsides to cast us wrathfully down; quite the
contrary, we gaze at the bank strewn with empty milk
cartons and tin cans and we recognize the limits Nature
has placed upon our consumption. In springtime all will
be revealed. The sun, a pale patch in the sky, and only a
handful of species remaining on earth. The air is very
dry. The woman's breath freezes as it leaves her lips, and
she holds a corner of her pink nylon dressing-gown to
her mouth. In principle, life has ample opportunities for
everyone.

The wind forces a frozen cry from her lips. An in-
voluntary and none too savage cry, a mute sound
squeezed out of her lungs. Helpless as the child, a field
tilled and ploughed and beaten till it's used to the
treatment. She cannot take her beloved child's side
against his father, because after all it was Father who
filled in the order form for extras such as music or
holidays. It's all behind her now. Her boisterous son is
probably tearing downhill into the dusky valley at this
very moment, like an upturned plastic ladybird in his
plastic moulded sledge. Soon everyone will be at home.
Eating. The terror of the day still pounding in their
hearts. If the child doesn't have pieces of shell stuck wet
behind his ears! Such filth. That children are here today
and gone tomorrow, like time, is the responsibility of
women, who stuff food into their own or Father's images

and show where things come out again. And, wielding
his sting, Father drives his sons out onto the piste, where
he can be lordandmaster of the leaderless mob.

The fist knocks the woman senseless against the railing.
She has left the last of the cottages far behind now. The
children's babble told clearly of how wonderful life is if
you let circumstances pull the wool over your eyes. With
eyes wide open, the woman always has to go walking on
other paths, she's always been squeezed from the tube of
her house into the open. Quite often she's gone astray.
She's lost her way a time or two and ended up at the
police station. Where the officers opened their arms wide
and welcomed her in, offering a place to rest. The poor
folk who spend too long at the pub get a different
welcome. Now Gerti is silent. Amid the elements. Which
soon will lie wide open beneath the stars. The child who
has been singled by Fate as her surviving next of kin is
boisterously tobogganing down the tracks left by others,
shooting a breeze of his own creation. Those who have
some notion of what's what prefer not to cross his path,
not to cross him. But Mother, impelled on her travels by
his will, travails from valley to valley to buy him
something. Now she is like a sleepwalker. Gone. The
villagers stroke her image behind the panes and try to
meet her so that she will put in a good word. The Orff
courses for infants, which the little ones try hard and
often to get out of, guarantee their fathers work at the
factory. The children are left as a deposit. They rattle and
bash their drums and cymbals and recorders. Why?
Because the goodly hand of their caring lordandmaster
who owns the factory, a sheltering place for one and all,
has staked them out as bait. At times the Direktor stops
by and dandles the little girls in his lap. He toys with the
hems of their skirts, ahem, and plays with their dolly
tea-cosy dresses, isn't this cosy, but doesn't dare wade
any deeper in their waters. Still, everything happens
under his guardian hand. The children clatter away on

the air holes of their musical instruments. And lower down, where there are openings in their bodies, a terrible finger comes out softly into the clearing, as if in its sleep. And not till an hour later will the children be safe in the breath of their mothers. Suffer the children to come, so that the family can take their supper in a merry atmosphere in the sunshine in the glow of gleaming classical records. And the teacher, as soon as the children crowd into the room, sits totally silent in her compartment, beyond the window of which the station-master goes on moving his lips till her train has left.

The Direktor approves of everything his wife does. And she puts up with his ever-ready meat battery. Slotted home to light up her health. He seems almost amazed to find his natural fertilizer enriching her well-ploughed field time and again. To have his load crash time after time upon the deck of her ship. From her sleeves, in alarm, comes intermittent piano music, only to fade and die again. The children don't understand a thing. Except that their bellies are being stroked and their tender inner thighs. These unmusical creatures have not learnt any foreign languages. From the corners of their bored eyes they glimpse the outside, where they can idle their time away undisturbed. The Direktor is on his way back from the heavenly choir where their fathers idle their time away disturbed. And the thunderous god's fingertips cling tight to the strawberries that have already started to ripen in their cold, hard beds.

It drives the Man nuts, he's white-hot and could crush flies in his fingers at the thought of it: this tiny start that even children have on him, which he has driven out of his wife's body with just two fingers, so he can clamber up and be king of the castle. Just having the woman at his disposal isn't enough. He has to spread out in her. Act the lout. Make himself at home. Put his feet up. Let's face it, what he wants is to hide away in her and get a little peace.

Now and then, still trembling with the heavy, droning beat of his wings of flesh, he offers an almost apologetic apology to this gentle creature upon whom he cannot impress his stamp, even though he has gobbled and spat out every millimetre of her flesh. Preposterous, really, to be ashamed of a decent day's work on the marital job!

When night has nearly fallen there are some who go from village to village in their vehicles, a spawn of stereo speakers squelching music about their brains. One driver, a guest in his vehicle, pulls over by the woman. The pebbles of the forest road fly from his tyres. Most men are more familiar with their cars' biographies than with their wives' autobiographies. What, it's the other way round with you? You know yourself as well as you know the simple person who revives and restores you every day anew? The light of your life, slinging out your used rubbers? Then count yourself fortunate and sit down!

Now will all of those who want to drink all night please stand up and go to the back! The rest who would rather drink to the small hours, small talk, bed talk, till they have the affection of another, stay put. Night is there for the sole purpose of draining the bottle of youth. Which kicks and yells in its glossy mag nappies. Now at last youngsters can smash the glass vessel the schnapps drips from, the light bulb of their upbringing, the backs of their hands will be marked in discos and their faces by steel bridge railings. That's the way of the world. Right inside us. Unemployed youngsters are chary of the road into free open spaces. Warily they torment small animals they have managed to get in their power, in soundless hutches. No one will take them at the garages and the glitzy hairdressing salons in town. The paper mill pretends to be asleep too, to avoid any social dilemma when the village lads, wings folded shut and heads retracted, smash into it. Because they would like to stir the paper pulp along with the others. But what they actually do is to drink too deeply. They're already wearing their Sunday best on weekdays. Anyone who has a small holding back home is the first to be slung out of the factory and keeps his wife busy back home. He seems to be self-sufficient in food and to reap a harvest of divine plenty. Anyone who slaughters animals in private cannot have his heart entirely in the factory, declares the personnel manager. Either one thing or the other. The children fall ill. The fathers hang themselves. No money on earth can ever pay them what they're owed.

There he goes. Driving by in his very own car across the frozen earth, right by the woman. Young though he is, he has already passed his finals in justice and life in the fast lane. He still has parents too, though he doesn't need to bother about them, by the long and dusty road a senior employee has to travel on the way to getting his face on the Austrian People's Party campaign poster. That way is as long as ours from the door to the heating or newspaper, which make things so comfortable for us in this medium-income-group state. His parents have bought a weekend home here fairly painlessly, with a bank loan. The house is available for rest, for sport, and for resting before and after sport. Unlike them, this man is a member of an exclusive student fraternity where the aristocracy thaw open the eyes of the middle classes and promptly gum them shut again. What this fellow can't do isn't worth mentioning in the Vienna Young Athletes' Association circular. His is a non-duelling fraternity but the fraternizing is hearty. Heartlessly the small fry get their knives into each other. But meanwhile the big boys are casting a bright light and climbing their way to the top, amid the mighty shadows that chart their progress, stepping on the hands and heads of the rest; and presently they relax their bowels, and their sails fill with the wind they pass. You don't see them coming. But suddenly there they are, in parliament, in the government.

Just as with agricultural products, which don't poison you till they're off the shelf and in your guts.

The woman has to stop. It has been snowing day and night. The mountain air hurts. The rays that fell through the trees have vanished now. The young man brakes so abruptly that a number of books that have long since turned against him fall upon him. They tumble into the legroom in front of the passenger seat. The woman peeks in at the window and sees a head that was legless last night, a skull that got a skinful like the hopeless folk around here under whose feet the earth is steaming. They know each other slightly by sight but neither has ever taken mental note of the other. The student reels off various expensive names she ought to know. The lofty peaks about them glisten in their caps of snow, the snow reaches the whole way down, to the workshop depths where humanity is busy crafting wishes for a new set of skis.

Meanwhile the Direktor is waiting in his office, and won't be any help to us if we go pounding at his door. The farm lads' dads have thrashed them black and blue, the cows at home are black and white and that's how they see the world, and here they are, braving a first step into the poorest-paid group of industrial workers. Soon they become aware of women. They bark and woof when they see women in cars varnishing their nails at a red light. They are the unimportant guests at the set table, invited so that they will see in good time just how unwelcome their intrusion into the yielding fabric of society is. From where they sit they can't even see all the social burdens that are heaped on the groaning table. There they sit, on the seats of their leather shorts, yawping to find their member of parliament already sitting there, wanting to drink their life juice concentrate straight from the can. Sons of the earth, they seem. Made to love and suffer. But a mere year later all they want to do is drive fast, be it a moped or a used Volkswagen, so the hair flies about their heads. And the river flows jauntily along beside them, finally to receive them with no questions asked.

The woman is so tired. As if she, complete with her still passable figure, which is usually covered by her husband, were about to topple over forward. The eyes of the world are upon her, at every step that she takes. She is buried among her possessions, which heave high aloft, foaming with conditioner, from one lowly horizon to the next. Then along come the busybody villagers and their valiant dogs, scraping and scratching at her doings till a thousand conversations have dug her up. Scarcely one of them could say what she looks like. As for what she's wearing, though! If only all those voices were uplifted on Sunday in church! A thousand little voices, flames flickering heavenward from the dusky workshop where the daily papers have done the preparation and fashioned people into clay vessels. The Direktor is cock of the walk. The women of the village are merely side-dishes to go with their husbands' meat. No, I do not envy you. And the men, like chaff, like dry hay, fall upon the computer-printed slips which record their fates plus the overtime they have to work if they're to strike up the happier tunes of life. No time to have fun with the kids after work. The newspapers turn like weathervanes in the wind, whether the employees of the paper mill sing or not it's all in vain. Back at school they all did well, I can't figure it out. They must forget it all later when they become figures in the business, commercial or industrial statistics, or black holes in the sporting universe. Word is passed to them of the games young people play the whole world over, but by the time it reaches them it's too late and they're slithering down the gentle slope outside their house, not that it takes them anywhere but another icy path to the tobacconist's on the corner where they find out who won. They watch it all on TV. They want to be bottled as deliciously as that too. Sport is their holy of holies, the holiest thing they can lay their fettered hands on. It's like the dining car on a train, not an absolute necessity but a way of combining the useless with the unpleasant. And, after all, you're getting somewhere.

The Direktor's wife is expected to get in out of the dark, into this car, so that she doesn't catch cold. She is not expected to make a fuss. Nor to carry on the way women like to carry on, when they first serve up dinner to their families and then spoil it for them with their nagging. All day long a man lives off the beautiful image of his wife, only to have her nag all evening. From the private boxes of their battlemented windows, where window boxes of flowers and plants form a spiky defence against the world, they look down at others who draw the bow too tight and relax their own longings out of sheer exhaustion. They put on their party best, cook for three days ahead, leave the house, and throw themselves, as you make your bed so you must lie on it, into the nearest reservoir or river.

The student notices the woman is wearing slippers. Helping others is his job. There she stands on her paper-thin soles. One of the legion of henpeckers who spend their lives eating leftovers spurned by the family. She takes a swig from a pocket edition of a bottle which is held to her lips. She and the village women and all of us, there we stand, dripping and thawing, facing the kitchen stove and counting the tablespoonfuls in which we dole ourselves out. The woman whispers something to the young man, she's picked a right one here, a right wing one at that, who's often fraternized till he was drunk in a heap on the floor. He returns her gaze. At the slightest stir of feeling, her sleepy head is already resting on his shoulder. The car tyres rasp, wanting to be off. An animal stands up, hearing its cue, and the young man too wouldn't be averse to rummaging in this woman's cast-offs for a little small change. For a change. It would be something different, naughty, unexpected. Afterwards you could drape a flimsy cloak of talk about the encounter. His fellows at the fraternity have long since bagged their first quarries, and the fleeces, once combed and cared for by loving mothers, are hung about their shoulders. Now at last one's own wishes, straining impatiently at the leash, can be tossed something nourishing to eat, meat cut out of another. So that those wishes grow big and strong. And one day have big fishes in the ocean of the top management floors dancing attendance. Yes, Nature means business. And happily we chain her up, to score against her will if need be. Futile for the elements to roar. We are already in the waves!

7

ALL AROUND, OPPRESSED people are falling, cascades of water, down steps and ornate porches into the uncertain consciences of their oppressors. Tame-spirited creatures that they are, they don't overshoot the mark. Every morning the boisterous radio bawls that it's time to get up, wakey wakey. And instantly the warmth of love is yanked away from under their feet and their sweat-soaked sheet taken from them. They grope about their wives, they dirty their precious belongings. Time breezes gently by. People have to fulfil their pensum before they can draw a pension. Before they are paid off. And have themselves paid off the things they believed — their whole lives long, with eyes tight shut — they owned. Just because they were tolerated among those things as visitors. While their wives, by using them constantly, coaxed the things into life. Only women are really at home. The men loaf oafishly in the under-growth at night. Or leap about the dance floor. The paper mill. The mill spews people out, after they've been of use for years. But first they go to the top floor to collect their papers.

The Frau Direktor dwells in their midst. Quiet. White. Not even a good roast will set her up to go on living as it does with you and me. The children are brought to her to learn to rattle and prattle. Till the sustaining sound of music falls silent and the howl of the factory is upraised across the mountaintops. Early in the mornings the fathers sleepily splash their jets into the toilet, while apprentices are more rudely awakened, with music dinned into them the moment their alarms go off. The half-naked bodies grow in front of the mirrors in the newly-tiled bathrooms. The chains gleam. The little cocks crow merrily from the flies, the warm waters are passed. Perhaps this toilet is a mirror image of you. So

please leave it in the same condition that you would like
to be left in!

A car is parked in front of the Direktor's wife. An animal
gazes out from within itself and bounds into the wood,
where it has its peace and quiet. True: in summer, the
heavily-laden rafts of life float there. People off to
unload in Nature. To relieve themselves. The car is
warm, suddenly the sky seems much lower down. Time
is tending to a close and people get close and grow tender.
In the wood, the deer, who have an even worse time of it
in winter than we do, stretch. The woman cries, leaning
on the dashboard, and fumbles in the glove compartment
for a handkerchief to dry her misery. The car starts.
Questions are scattered around like gifts. Right away,
the woman throws open the door of the car as it's
moving off and plunges into the wood. She is full to the
brim with her feelings, fit to burst, and she has to give
vent to her instincts, like steam escaping through a vent,
hiss, boo hiss, boo hoo, boo his, boo whose? That is what
the books say; because you value yourself, you can buy
one of these cheap books and read all about it. As if she'd
run into a swarm of gnats or some other unfamiliar mob,
the woman waves her arms about, trips over a root, cuts
her face on hard old snow and vanishes into the darker
part of the wood. No, there she goes! Stumbling over the
twisted black branches. Whereupon she returns of her
own free will to the leash and strap, gets into the car, and
is bedded down into the leisurely depth of the seat.
Within herself she grows. And is at her own service. She
can hear her feelings rumbling closer like thunder.
Racing like an express through the station of her body.
Even the station-master's slender signal baton is almost
too much for her. She is obeying her own command. And
no one else's. The powerful current that charges these
creatures of feeling shocks them like divine intervention.
How wonderful are the people with enough time to
acquire a pilot's licence for their own rudderless, drifting

feelings, so they can fly hither and thither within themselves!

In the midst of her life, this woman often likes to think she has to get out of her alignment alongside other women with sagging breasts and hopes who have docked beside her. Get out and away to a sumptuous land where tears are dried with greater care. She is fond of herself to the point of idolatry. A package tourist in the country of circumspect passions. Fixing assignations with herself wherever she chooses. And fleeing herself at the same time, because somewhere else she might enjoy an even more thrilling rendezvous with her inner self. Somewhere that you can sit on a cloud and quaff even more deeply from the golden goblets of your own emotion. She is as volatile as a compound that will dissolve at any moment.

Likewise with art and what we feel about it. Everyone feels differently. Most people feel nothing at all. And yet we're agreed on scraping the bottom of our barrel and serving up what we find, only half done, for the others to devour. The flames roar from our little stoves, you'd think we were getting on like a house on fire. Down we go, in all too rapid pursuit of our desires, as if we were on ice. The sun shines, and the rooms where we stew in our lust for life are well heated too. Everything is hot, and the spirit, warmed by licking flames, rises high above us for others to see. Sooner or later we take a tumble because we don't have our feet on the ground any more, we're in love and the demands we make on our partners are groundless. How happy we are to go romping about the mountains, as infinitely various as creation, till we lose our pointed caps.

On his high and mightily expensive horse, the student lends an ear as the woman places herself in his hands. A once-only occasion has led her into the hallway of her sensibility. The silence is steamy with feverish talk, like a hot-house. Bundled into words, the days of her child-hood and the lies of her adulthood shoot shuddering from the woman. The student is led down the slope of her thoughts. The woman goes on talking to make herself more important, and her words part company with truth at the very moment when the truth dawns on her and seems bright as day. Whoever listens, anyway, when a housewife heads into the interior because the child is screaming or the food has caught light. The more the woman talks and talks, the more she wishes that she and this man could remain unknown quantities for each other, just interesting enough to afford each other a little rest along the way, so that they didn't have to leap to their feet and instantly be up and running again.

But who can rival the senses for feeling pain? In rattling pots, with the steam lifting the lid to sing out, we cook our emotions. But what of those battered by the threat of redundancy? They bang their heads against the wall of the paper mill, which the mother company may have to write off because it isn't turning any profits. And in any case it pollutes the stream, and there are now a fair number, clumsily sharpening their claws, who listen to the voice of Nature. Nature having finally learnt the language of her children. These people, bred at institutes of higher education, understand what Nature is saying and what goes on in her air and waters. When they argue, a smile spreads across their faces, because they are in the right. Nature, like their feelings, is entirely of their opinion. Samples of ill-bred, loutish water are carefully tended and nurtured by environmentalists, but somewhere or other a new wound will gash wide open in Nature and they'll have to go hurrying off to it. After a while the human waste comes shooting out at both ends. It was already muck when it went in. That's it: with local help, the mill has created paper, our very own fertilizer, on which, creasing bloody wrinkles into the sofas where we lie, we can even write down our thoughts. Whatever we have to say to each other — the sweet nothings and sweet nights of love with which we hope to grow monstrous specimens of ourselves on the manure of our loved ones — whatever we have to say, it makes no impression on our partner, who is occupied with other thoughts that have to be rinsed out and filled up every day anew.

The more profound people's happiness, the less they speak of it in these parts, so that they don't lose their way in it and the neighbours aren't envious. Those who are cast out by the factory have to cast about for somewhere they can get credit from those on whose largesse and mercy they cast themselves. In the darkness dwell their lordsandmasters, the eagles, who can change their prey's fate with a single nod of the ballpoint. But the lusty sons of the Alps stride out fearlessly across the flimsy bridges that span ravines, off they go to visit their relatives, striding out fearlessly to the wimps and bitches, coffee and ice cream, coffin and I scream, the horror. Fearful stuff, but they don't notice what they feel and don't listen if it's explained to them.

The young man leans across to the woman, who has withdrawn a little to natter with her nearest and dearest, her secret dreams and longings. From her big eyes the tears well up and fall into her lap. Where desire abides, biding its time, clipping its nails. We're not animals, after all. Things don't always have to happen right away. First we ponder whether he's a suitable partner for us and we wonder what he can afford before we spurn him. Now our cup floweth over, we are all there, though it's taken all these years. You just have to remember to swim on the surface of the water, so that you can watch the other boats in the distance and see who they've invited and incited, while they for their part watch at leisure as you go under. In a swimsuit, what's more, from which pert parts of your body, parts that would best be kept hidden, peek cheekily out. No one knows his body, his house, his many mansions, better than the owner does. But that doesn't mean you can go inviting people in. Why should another man not love us? And why, then, does he not do so?

The young man slips the dressing-gown off Gerti's shoulder. The woman cannot come to terms, she squirms, she worms about on her seat as if she needed more space. Tenderly though her inmost self is calling from her cleavage, it wants to stay in, where it is, and maybe take a stroll out where the trees are (what else). Gerti has barely escaped the safety belt of her house but this young man of law wants to grope in her glove box. To think how many cavities there are in a healthy body! And, heavens, in an unhealthy one! The woman bares her soul and her bosom with words. And the student will get his chance to pinion her with opinions and shove his love into her. At last, Michael has stopped his car at an enclosure where you can feed the game. She's game. The powers that be and their forestry workers like to lay out these enclosures, each a manmade paradise where Nature, clumsy, all thumbs, can enter in. And women are promised paradise if only they will create it on this earth for their husbands and children and season it properly. And the seasons go by without a moment's respite, to torment them.

From the woman, hopes the young man, a stream of longing and desire will flow. Lying contentedly on his stomach, he pokes the ants out of their hill with his stick. The tiny creatures are fast, they're coaxed out and scatter in every direction. They're hard to catch, but at times they come of their own accord, like dreams. Then you can add an extra load, even your big log. Bodies have to be kept alight. We use everything we've got to make sure they are. Just to keep our members atremble and our genitals at-it-againital. We can't let it be, we always have to be setting fire to things with our lighter. Trunks that used to seem safe have to be felled too, purely so that we can spread our arms open wide and cook and gobble life again, which we have been given as a gift in any case. And the dribs and drabs of women's lives, the rivulets that presently run dry, are always looking for some other torrent, as mighty as can be, to flow along in. Signals of love, a whole corps of them, flags run up poles. And troughs where animals dip their tongues or are done out of their own fluids by electrical gadgetry.

The stuff that Gerti's dreams are made on is torn from her shoulders and crumpled on the floor. She spills out her ruined life over this Son of Man, who only wants to feel her up and fill her up as fast as he can. Stubbornly she stays stuck in the nest of light the car provides. And tries to stand up again. Hop off into the life she's just come in from. On the roof that affords shelter for their bodies, skis are securely strapped in place on a rack. And she is insecurely on a rack. Here they are, two lovers, together, forever ready and willing to take a tumble off the ladder of emotion if something in their partner's beatific eyes isn't what they ordered off the menu. In a while they'll be getting better acquainted. And they'll be better at balancing platefuls of fate.

In the car it is so pleasantly warm that the blood shimmers in their bodies. By now, Nature is a gaping emptiness. In the distance, no children are screaming to their hearts' content. Right now they are screaming to their hearts' discontent in the punitive rooms of cottages where the hail of their fathers falls suddenly upon them. It's dark early and the women get their husband's full pay packet in their hands, here, cop a hold of this. Outside, your breath freezes on your chin. This mother is already being sought by her nearest and fearest. Her Almighty, the mill Direktor, that horse of immense physique, still steaming with roast, wants to wrap his arms and legs about her. Peel her fruit impatiently. Lick the juice. Before he rams his ever-ready in. His battering ram. Salt and battery, very tasty, the woman's good enough to eat. He could go for her lower half, he'd wolf her down, still steaming, with some of his own sauce to taste. Between his thighs his member waits, not stupid, this one. His bag hangs heavy, not long and he'll be unloading into her bowed head. One woman may even be enough for the Man, tumescent though he be with greed. He wants to go knocking his giblets at her nether regions to see if anyone's home. Reluctantly her lips will part, they definitely will part, and he'll compare them with other similar lips he knew once upon a time. In any case, this man prefers oral and anal sex. What can you do but cool off, remove your cap, shake out your locks, and dive in cheerfully? No one goes astray. And there are no dying echoes.

The Direktor's wife is envied by most other women in these parts, heavy-hipped women with great pelvic basins into which their menfolk, feet in hot water, open their veins and sluices. These hefty mares have only one way of becoming the chosen ones: they can cook up a home from garbage and rubble. Their figs grow out into the yard, but their menfolk like to go watering other furrows. And the women stay at home and wait for the magazines to show them how good they have it. Snug and dry in the disposable diapers of their wretched housework. But ah, what happiness — their kindly riders so like to get astraddle their saddles!

8

IN ALL SERIOUSNESS I call upon you: air and lust for one and all!

The woman will be with you in a moment, can you hold? First she has to collect herself: for a kiss it'd be best to be collected, all five senses, collect the set. The student is well developed, a perfect picture of a man, no need for touching up, so she lets him touch her up. He places his arm between her thighs. With his eye on the way ahead and the main chance, he rummages under her clothes, which consist chiefly of a plain dressing-gown, which won't be in the way for long. Many have to take terrible buses and regret it terribly when they remain on the wrong genitals for too long. The owner, or rather the passenger of his three-in-one wishes, grows too used to us and won't let us out of his ground-level hospitable apartment. Let me explain that three-in-one: Woman is a trinity of pleasures, to be grabbed up top, down below, or in the middle! Till at length they can move on to various amiable kinds of sport, possessing each other without understanding. Bawling and brawling. The woman is eager for the driver to drive her around a little, step on it.

It can't simply be because the toilet's in the corridor that we feel impelled to go out at night and, in front of the door, look slyly around to see if anyone's watching as we stand there with our hands to our sex, as if we might be due to lose it before we can place it in its hand-painted chipboard box.

Of the many kinds of accommodation he might choose, the young man opts for this one alone. But the closet won't keep still, no, it's even hurrying off ahead in the dark and the cold! This Gerti beats him to the enclosure. Many a one has talked of kissing here. Spread their torchlight wide. And cast great shadows on the walls, so that for one other person they will be greater than just anyone, just anyone on a ski lift. As if sheer carnal desire could make them greater, bigger! As if they could draw themselves up so erect that they'd slam the ball straight in the basket! Players can be mighty fine specimens, tall and erect, and there they stand before their partners, fully equipped, with all the necessary tackle. So many requirements, all of them pressing, pressed into the service of hygiene and filth alike, simply to possess each other. As the phrase inaptly goes. This dusty junk shop's where we end up. Two household objects. Of simple geometrical design. Wanting to fit together and be good as new again! Now! Suddenly there's a woman in combinations in the corridor, a jug of water in her hand; has she been casting spells, calling forth a storm, or is she only going to make some tea? In no time at all a woman can make a home of the plainest, barest, most spartan of places. That is to say, even the plainest of women can make a man feel at home by baring all, in no time he places his spar. This young man who has entered her life might be the great intellectual? Now everything will be different from how it was planned. We'll make a new plan on the spot. Our heads will swell good and proper. Oh, your boy plays the violin as well? But not at this very moment, surely, since no one's punching his start button.

Come on, she yells to Michael. As if she were demanding money of a shopkeeper who hates us customers. And yet he can't get by without us. He has to tempt us into his store or go penniless. Now the woman wants a pleasure that lasts at last. First of all, one! two! (you can do it too, sitting in your car, your speed as limited as your mental horizons) we lunge at each other's mouths, then we plunge into all the other orifices; in thy orifices may I be remembered. And all of a sudden our partner means everything to us. Presently, in a minute or two, Michael will penetrate Gerti, whom he hardly knows and has barely taken a look at. Just as a sleeping car attendant always knocks first with a hard object. He lifts the woman's dressing-gown over her head and with his mouth, in an excitement of his own creation, prompts her who was without form and void to make a frightful commotion in the queue. The queue at the cash desk where we're all waiting, money clenched and balled behind our flies. We are our own worst enemies in matters of taste. People all like different things, isn't that so? But what if we want to be liked? What will we do, in our infinite indolence: call upon sex to do the work for us?

Michael yanks the woman's legs about him like the legs of high-tension masts. In his exploratory zeal he gives intermittent attention to her undouched cleft, a gnarled version of what every other woman has on her person in a discreet shade of lavender or lilac. He pulls back and takes a good look at the place where he is repeatedly disappearing, only to reappear, a huge great thing, fun for one and all. A funster, this fellow. But flawed. Sport being one of his flaws, and hardly the least. The woman is calling him. What's got into him? Why hasn't it got into her? Since Gerti didn't have an opportunity to wash, her hole looks murky, as if it were plastic-coated. Who can resist jamming a finger in (you can use peas, lentils, safety pins or marbles if you like), try it and see what an enthusiastic response you'll get from your lesser half. Woman's unyielding sex looks as if it were unplanned. And what is it used for? So that Man can tussle with Nature, and the children and grandchildren have some-where to come trailing their clouds of glory from. Michael scrutinizes Gerti's complicated architecture and yells like a stuck pig. As if he were dissecting a corpse, he seizes her hairy cunt, stinking of secret dissatisfaction and dissatisfied secretions, and buries his face in it. You tell a horse's age by the teeth. This woman isn't so young any more either, but nonetheless this wrathful bird of prey is flapping at her door.

Michael laughs: he's terrific. Will we ever learn from these transactions? Will the one ever be able to cross the gap to the other, to talk and be understood and understand? Women's genitals, so outrageously located in a hillside, tend to be quite distinct, claims the expert. Just as no two people are entirely alike. They can wear quite different headgear, for instance. And the ladies are particularly prone to difference. No two of them are entirely alike. Not that a lover cares, when they lie prone: what he sees is what he's used to seeing on other women. In the mirror he sees himself reflected, his own deity. In the waters' depths. Fishing, plenty of fish in the sea, just hang out your dripping rod and wait for a catch, another woman to toss off your godhead in and then toss back. Ah, the privy parts and privy arts of mankind! All that's required of womankind is that she reck his rod (not wreck his rod), rock his godhead, toss his rocks off.

Let observation with extended view survey mankind . . . and what you'll see is the gaping gawp of somebody's integrated, semi-conducted craving for ecstasy. Go ahead. Try for something of real value! Feeling, perhaps, that guide who takes the tour party into terrain he's unfamiliar with, burgeoning through your skull? We don't have to watch him grow. We can choose another pupil to waken and give us pleasure. Yet the ingredients are stirred as we are. Our dough rises, puffed up with the sheer force of air, the atomic cloud mushrooming over the mountaintop. A door slams shut. And we're on our own again. Gerti's jolly husband, who is forever dangling his hose with a nonchalant air, as if his waters sprang from some precious source, isn't here right now to reach out his hand to his wife or torment his offspring on the rack of music. The woman laughs out loud at the thought. The young man is ramming his piston forcefully home, every stroke an attempt to get a little locomotion going, stoke her engine, can't you hear that whistle blow? He is taking a lively interest at present. Well aware of the changes even the least likely of women can undergo at the hands of a red-hot fresh and scented wad of male sex. Sex is the downtown of our lives, shopping precinct and leisure centre and red light district all in one, but it isn't where we live. We prefer a little elbow room, a bigger living room, with appliances we can turn on and off. Within her, this woman has already done an about-turn and is heading straight back for her own familiar allotment where she can pick the fruits of sensuality from her private plot herself and do the job with her own hands. Even alcohol becomes volatile at a certain point. But still, almost blubbing with joy at the changes he has wished upon himself, the young man is rummaging about the cosy taxi. He even looks under the seat. He opens Gerti, and then snaps her shut again. Nothing there!

Of course we can don hygienic caps if we like, to avoid the risk of disease. Otherwise, we have everything we need. And though the lordsandmasters cock their legs and slash their waters into their women, they can't remain but must hurry on, restless, to the next tree, where they waggle their genital worms till someone takes an interest. Pain flashes like lightning into women, but it does no permanent damage, no need to cry over charred furniture or molten appliances. And out it dribbles once again. Your partner will be willing to forgo anything but your feelings. After all, she likes to cook up feelings too. Poor people's food. I'd even say she's specialized in economy cooking, she's out to have men's hearts in a preserve jar at last. The poor prefer to turn away without being shoo'd about by tour guides. Their pricks even lay them down to rest before they do. And the source from which their waters spring is the heart. They leave the sheet unstained, and off we go.

At any rate, there are glasses that contain nothing of any greater sense than the wine. The Direktor likes looking into the glass: when it's raised to his lips he can see the bottom, and similarly he wants to drain his own immense tank, right into Gerti. The moment he sees her he exposes himself. His rain comes pouring from the cloudburst before she has a chance to run for shelter. His member is big and heavy and would fill the pan if you added his eggs. In the old days he used to invite many a woman to breakfast, they gobbled him up, slipped down a treat, but now he no longer calls in the hungry folk to eat at his table. Deformed by the opulence of leisure, humanity reclines in its deckchairs, resting its sex, or else strolls the gravel paths, sex in its pockets, hands in its pockets. Work restores humankind and all its attributes to the savage animal condition that was its original intended state. Thanks to one of Nature's whims, men's members are usually too small by the time they've got the knack of handling them. And there they go, leafing through the catalogues of exotic women, high-performance models that are more economical to run and need less fuel. The dipsticks plunge their dipsticks in the sump they know best, which happens to be their wives. Whom they wouldn't trust as far as they could throw them. So they stay home to keep a watch on them. Then their gaze pans across to the factory in the mist. Though, if they applied themselves a little more patiently, they could take a holiday as far afield as the Adriatic. Where they could dip their sticks in other waters. Their gangling danglers, carefully packed in their elasticated bathing trunks. Their wives wear sawn-off swimsuits. Their breasts are close friends, but they also like making new acquaintances, how do you do, a firm grip, perhaps too firm, uncouthly dragging them from the recliners where they were lounging, lazy and tender, tearing them out, crumpling them in careless fingers and tossing them into the nearest wastepaper basket.

*

There are signposts along the roads, pointing the way to the towns. Only this woman has to go messing about where children are trying to get their first bearings in life. Calm down and carry on! Hereabouts it is distinctly frosty and foresty. There's a smell of hay. Of straw. Strewn for us, for the animal within. The dog in the manger. How often we've taken the mangy creature walkies! How many before us — who would gladly have buried their wives if they could harvest a goodly crop of women from the place — have splashed and sprayed here! Like winning a motor race! Or like giving it all away: someone, for instance, has thrown a condom away before turning homeward once again. Most men have no idea what you can perform on that keyboard, the clitoris. But they've all read the magazines that prove there's more to women than anyone ever imagined. A milli-metre or so more, to be exact.

The student crushes the woman to him. The hissing that escapes from his pent valve can be stopped by the merest touch, he can do it himself. He doesn't want to squirt off yet, nor does he want the wait to have been in vain. As she reclines there in his upholstered crate, he clumsily paws and pinches the most unseemly parts of the woman's anatomy, so that she has to spread her legs further apart. He rummages in her slumbering sex, squeezes it into a pout and smacks it abruptly apart again. Oughtn't he to excuse himself, given that he's treating her worse than the furniture? He slaps her derrière and heaves her onto her back once more. He'll sleep well tonight, that's for sure, like anyone who's done an honest day's work and then taken his innocent rest and recreation.

His hands clawed tight in her hair, the student quickly fucks the woman shitless, it messes the car seats but what the fuck. As he services her, he does not look out at the world, where only the beautiful come in for care and maintenance, a major service every few thousand miles. He looks at her, trying to read something in that face which has been rendered indecipherable by her husband. Men are capable of detaching themselves from the world for as long as they want. Only to take a tighter grip on their own tour group afterwards. They have the option. Everyone who has any idea about men knows who we mean: that male world, a couple of thousand people involved in sport, politics, the economy, the arts. Where the rest come a cropper. And who will love them all, that crop of puffed-up flatulent bigmouths? What does the student see, beyond his own body's unctions and functions? The woman's mouth, a source from which streams well up, and the floor, from where her image laughs at him. They don't bother with any rubber protection. The man half turns away in order to watch his rigid member entering and exiting. The woman's socket gapes wide. The piggy bank squeaks, it's designed for paying in, only to pay everything promptly out again. Both transactions are of equal importance in this business, but you try telling that to any modern businessman, he'll raise his eyebrows in alarm, he'll raise the alarm, he'll lift his kids up high so that they don't step in their inferiors' anger.

Gradually the spasms the man has set going in the woman calm and subside. She's had hers and perhaps she'll even get a second helping. Quiet! Now only the senses are doing the talking. But we don't understand what they're saying, because under the seat they've changed into something incomprehensible.

The student spills his packetful into the animals' cratch, fills his packet into the animal's snatch. Now it is deepest night. Clad in deepest black. Elsewhere, people are turning over, thinking of other more finely built specimens they've seen in magazines before they dock their bodies alongside for love. When Michael unbuckled his skis, he didn't pause to consider that sport, that eternal constant of our world, which hath its dwelling place in the TV set, doesn't simply stop when you've shot down your slope. The whole of life is sport. Sports dress enlivens our existence. All our relatives under the age of eighty wear tracksuits and T-shirts. Tomorrow's eggs are on sale today so you can count your chickens before they're hatched. There are others who are better-looking or cleverer than we are, for it is written. But what will become of those of whom no mention at all is made? And their inactive unattractive penises: where shall they channel their little rivers? Where is the bed for them to flow and lay their heads to rest? On this earth they are forever worrying about their wretched little organs, but where oh where shall they spray the anti-freeze to afford protection in the winter to come, so their engines don't refuse to start? Will they negotiate union, or negotiate with a union? What ridges and ranges of perfumed flesh strew the path of dalliance, all the way till the stock feel the knife on the throat and the family feel the ramrod and the lash? For those who are attractive, and who generally tend to be the most active too, are not mere décor in our lives. They want to plug their members into other people's sockets, any will do. Always bear in mind that, in their attempt to get what they want, people will hide away far inside each other, inseparable. So the atom doesn't split them.

Even before the minute hand of happiness can stroke the two of them, Michael has emitted a fluid, and that's it. But, in the woman, nuclear energy is powering her higher. These are the headwaters of which she has secretly dreamt for decades. Ah, the faithful old work-horse, pulling the man's body at the woman's whiplash behest! These forces are felt in even the tiniest remotest ramifications of the female. They spread like wildfire. The woman hugs the man tight as if he had become a part of her. She cries out. Presently, her head turned by what she feels, she'll be going on her way, dripping the seeds of discord in the petty principality of her household, and wherever the seed touches the earth mandrakes and other creatures will shoot up and grow, for her sake. This woman belongs to love. Now, for sure, she has to make certain she revisits this wonderful leisure centre. Again and again. Because this young man has hauled out his tool (now next to useless) and waved it about, see you again, Gerti suddenly sees his face with the pimple at the top right in a totally new and meaningful light. It is a face she'll have to see again, of course. Her future will depend on this go-getter's talent for gun-running, the secret arms trade hidden in his trousers. From now on, his one and only joy shall be to dwell inside Gerti. But here come the windy gusts. The breezy gusto. Bang on time. For holidays over the hills and far away are ruffling and dishevelling and tousling the desire of girls and women, so that they want a good hard regular brushing. In town, where you can go dancing in the cafés, the women on holiday congregate in deadened leaden droves. Ready to fall when night falls. Michael, who is interested in shooting off the lead in his pencil, will have to invest in rubber. And make his choice of the women dressed in their *après ski* best. All of them are natural beauties with natural tastes in natural sex, naturally, that's what he likes best. Make-up painted over pimples would blow him clean away.

Long before opening time, poor Gerti is sure to be at the telephone tomorrow, pestering it. This Michael, if the signals he's sending us and has himself received from various magazines can be relied on, is a blond creature off the cinema screen. Looking as if he'd been out in the sun for some time, with gel in his hair. Prompting us to finger our own sex, he's giving us the finger, he won't give us the finger for real. He is and always will be far away from us. Remote even when he's close. He enjoys night life. Keeping the night alive, lively. Not a man who cares for restraint. It's not easy to account for lightning, either: but in middle age we women are herded together in an enclosure of weekend assignations, and the bolt will strike one of us, that's for sure, before we have to leave.

Mind how you go. You may have something about your person that men like that would find a use for!

The animals are falling asleep, and desire has drawn Gerti out of herself, has struck a spark from her little pocket lighter, but where's this draught come from that's made the flame burn higher? From this heart-shaped peep-hole? From some other loving heart? In winter they go skiing, in summer they are the children of light, playing tennis or swimming or finding other reasons to undress, other smouldering fires to stamp out. When once a woman's senses are bespoke you can be sure she'll make other slips of the tongue. This woman hates her sex. Which once she was the finest flower of.

The simpler folk hidden away behind their front gardens will soon be silent. But the woman is crying out loud for her idol Michael, long promised her in photographs that look like him. He's just been for a fast drive in the Alps, now she roars and turns the vehicle of her body in every direction. It's a steep downhill stretch. But even as she lies there whining and pining the clever housewife is planning the next rendezvous with her hero, who will provide shade on hot days and warm her on cold. When will they be able to meet without the lugubrious shadow of Gerti's husband falling across them? You know how it is with the ladies: the immortal image of their pleasures means more to them than the mortal original, which sooner or later they will have to expose to life. To competition. When, fevering, chained to their bodies, they show up at a café in a new dress, to be seen in public with somebody new. They want to look at the picture of their loved one, that wonderful vision, in the peace and quiet of the marital wedroom, snuggled up side by side with the one who sometimes idly juggles his balls and pokes his poker in. Every one of these images is better accommodated in memory than life itself. On our own, we pick the memories from between our toes: how good it was to have properly unlocked oneself for once! Gerti can even bake herself anew and serve up her fresh rolls to the Man in the breadroom. And the children sing the praises of their Baker.

All of us earn the utmost we can carry.

The meadows are frozen entirely over. The senseless are beginning to think of going to bed, to lose themselves altogether. Gerti clings to Michael; let her climb every mountain, she still won't find another like him. In the school of life, this young man has often been a beacon of light to his fellows, who are already taking their bearings from his appearance and his nose, which can always sniff out the genuine article from among the column inches of untruth. Most of the houses hereabouts hang aslant the slope, the sheds and byres clinging on to the walls with the last of their strength. They have heard of love, true. But they never got round to the purchasing of property that goes with it. So now they're ashamed to be seen by their own TV screen. Where someone is just losing the memory game, the memory he wanted to leave with the viewers, the bill-and-cooers at home in their love-seats, hot-seats, forget-me-not-seats. Still, they have the power to preserve the image in their memories or reject it. Love it or shove it. Over the cliff. I can't figure it out: is this the trigger on the eye's rifle, this eyeful, is this the outrigger on the ship of courting senses, this sensitive courtship? Or am I completely wrong?

Michael and Gerti can't get enough of touching.

Necking. Checking to see if they're still there. Clawing and pawing each other's genitalia, done up in festive regalia as if for a première. Gerti speaks of her feelings and how far she'd like to follow them. Michael gapes as he realizes what he's landed. Time to get out the rod and go fishing again. He hauls the woman round by the hair till she's flapping above him like a great bird. The woman, awoken from the sedation of sex, is about to use her gob for uninhibited talking, but while it's open Michael can think of better things to do with it and shoves his corncob in, amazing. The woman's dragged by the hair against Michael's firm belly, then skewered face-first on Michael's shish-kebab. This continues for a while. Scarcely conceivable, that thousands of other insensate beings are wallowing in their misery at this very moment, forced by a terrible God to be parted from their loved ones all week long, in his illuminated factory. I hope your fate can be loosened a notch or two, so you can fit more in!

These two want to wonder and wander and squander each other, they have plenty of themselves in store and all the latest catalogues of erotica at home. Just think of those who don't need the expensive extras, who hold each other dear without the sundries! Their special offers are themselves. They flood their banks and dykes, they won't be dammed or damned, they go with the flow of experience, the tide takes them where it will. Suddenly Gerti has an irresistible urge to piss, which she does, first hesitantly, then full force. The vapour fills the confined space. She wraps the dressing-gown about her thighs and it gets wet. Michael playfully cups his hands and catches some of the audible jet, laughing he washes his face and body, then thumps Gerti onto her back and chews at her dripping labia, sucking and wringing out the rags. Then he drags Gerti into her own puddle and splashes her in it. She rolls her eyes upward but there's no lightbulb up there, just the darkness inside her

grinning skull. This is a feast. We're on our own, talking
to our sex: our dearest of guests, though one who is
forever wanting the choicest titbits. The dressing-gown,
which the woman has pulled back on again, is torn off
her once more, and she beds down deep in the hay. On
the floorboards there's a wet patch. As if some superior
being no one saw coming had made it. The only light is
moonlight. Illuminating the present. Expecting a present
in return.

The pallid bags of her breasts sag on her ribcage. Only
one man and one child have ever made use of them. The
Man back home ever bakes his impetuous daily bread
anew. If your breasts hang right down on the table at
dinner you can get an operation. They were made for the
child and for the Man and for the child in the Man. Their
owner is still writhing in her excreted fluid. Her bones
and hinges are rattling with cold. Michael, racing down
the slope, chomps at her privates and clutches and tugs at
her dugs. Any moment now his God-given sap will rise in
his stem, his cup will overflow. Hurry up, stuff that prick
in its designated slot, no loitering. You can hear her
shrieks, you can see the whites of her eyes, what are you
waiting for?

The young man is suddenly alarmed at the totality with
which he can spend himself without being spent. Again
and again he reappears from within the woman, only to
bury his little bird in the box again. He's now licked Gerti
from top to toe. His tongue's still tart with the taste of
her piss. Next her face. The woman snaps at him and
bites. It hurts, but it's a language animals understand. He
grabs her head, still by the hair, pulls it up off the floor
and slams it back where he first found it. Gerti splays her
mouth wide open and Michael's penis gives it a thorough
go. Her eyes are shut. He jabs his knees in, forcing the
woman to spread her thighs again. The novelty of this
has worn off, unfortunately, since he did it the same way

last time. So there you are, all skin and flick, and your desire is always the same old film! An endless chain of repetitions, less appealing every time because the electronic media and melodies have accustomed us to having something new home-delivered every day. Michael spreads Gerti wide as if he wanted to nail her to a cross and were not presently going to hang her in the wardrobe with the other clothes he rarely wears, which is what he'd actually intended. He stares at her cleft. This is familiar territory now. When she looks away, because she cannot bear his scrutiny and the groping, pinching hands that examine her, he hits her. He wants to see and do everything. He has a right to. There are details you can't see, and, in the event of there being a next time, a flashlight would come in handy. Before going in out of the night to the bodywork repairs shop. This woman had best learn to take the lordandmaster's examination of her sex. And not hang her feelings on his peg. For thereby hangs a tale.

Hay cascades over her, warming her slightly. The master is finished. The woman's wound is throbbing and swollen. Retracting his instrument abruptly, Michael signals that he wants to retire to the tidy quarters of his own body. Already he has become a platform for this woman, from which she will speak on the subject of her longing and his long thing. Thus, without so much as being photographed in undewear and framed, one can become the centre-piece of a well-appointed room. This young man created the white and awe-inspiring mountains of flesh before him. Like the evening sun, he has touched that face with red. He has taken a lease on the woman, and as far as she's concerned he can now grope under her dress whenever he likes.

Gerti covers Michael with soft and downy kisses. Soon she will return to her house and her lordandmaster, who has qualities of his own. For we always wish to return to the place of our old wounds and tear open the gift wrapping in which we have disguised the old as the new, to conceal it. And our declining star teaches us nothing at all.

9

THE WOMAN WHO RAN away is now returning, driven in a stranger's car, to her domestic bliss. To pick up her role in the home movie. As an eyecatching housewife. A drool of saliva slobbering off her chin is the first thing to catch her husband's eye. Now the young man is worried about her, having taken a brief look into her furthest distance and pressed his damp hands to her face. Now isn't the time, true, to lie out in the sun and show off one's body. Suddenly it's snowing again. Has the Direktor phoned the insurance, so that the woman can simply have him replaced with a younger model? In the old days he often came home straight from the brothel, where he'd had a hard time being idle. Washed, cut and laid. In the town whorehouse he used to pole his punt with impunity, but those days are over. Now he has to amuse his own wife, solo, with only his claws, two testicles, and an anus — for it is with such props that domestic entertainment is staged, when the child is unconscious. On reflection, he's a ponderous individual, even when he casts the image of his new tie in the mirror. He slams into his employees loud as a shout, and they play dumb, hoping it won't be me, not me, not me.

The house has already retired for the night by the time we get there. In one room only a worried light is still burning, for the precious child. Throwing up his surfeit of lessons all over his bed. In the boy's room, the Direktor ventures to get all his anger off his chest. This isn't his territory. He doesn't like hearing the water gush to fill the flush. He practically exploded when he found the empty bottles of cheap white wine yet again. Why can't she drink mineral water and be a loving mother for the child? He has forbidden her to drink, but she goes on zonking back the plonk. Has the cow been spreading her hind quarters for some other bull? He bows his lips above the child, so softly that he cannot get a word out. The child is asleep now. Without doing a thing, the boy provides an explanation of why the Direktor is alive. There he rests, mouth open, in the chest of his room. A room of their own is more than poor kids round here have ever even seen when they've been ill. Where is the child in this country who has a room his body will fit into? And where he can look at teddy bears and pictures of sport and pop stars? Because of the sexual ruckus of his parents, this boy has been transferred to a quiet spot. He's a dab hand, though, when it comes to keyholes. And good at ructions of his own, too, when he's beaten for wetting his pants. How he can howl.

It seems he has second sight, their son. Often he will materialize out of gloomy corners; his parents know no reticence in their bodily functions, they still believe in hard work! The Christian society that married them blessed their indulgence in that pleasure. Father has official permission to enjoy Mother ad infinitum, to raggle-taggle her rags and togs till her fear of revealing her secrets has been altogether overcome.

Those who are far away from us are lying abed, touch wood, that they may be well rested come daybreak. Too tired to be summoned by a dread God to the summit of time, to their loved ones, who die too soon. Tomorrow they will hurriedly bolt their breakfast and set off by bus to perform their paltry works; and the least of their works, the children, are sitting there beside them, because they have to go to school. The Direktor of the paper mill strides up to the extra biggest of big choir stalls. Those of his workforce who are awaiting the company pension keep politely to the rear. It's little short of a miracle that these people aren't mere animals, though they do live like animals, as their boss observes to his wife. Their pallid flaccid wives do not inspire them, so what we lordsandmasters call the breath of life is not in

them, too bad. Whoever would think that after holy
mass the Direktor pulls down his wife's panties and
inserts first one and then a second finger to check if the
waters are rising, how high they are now, up to her neck
yet? I wonder what is going on down below in other
women. Whatever it is, perhaps it would fancy a spell on
the surface to cuddle and canoodle.

Now all of us in this Roman Catholic country will go
down on our knees for a while so that all can see us
washing the blood of innocence off our hands, the blood
that God, making a superhuman effort, has transformed
into himself: man and woman, right, that was his work,
his doing. In readers' letters to the paper they are true
to themselves and each other, because they are true to
the spirit of Christian architecture, forever striving
heavenward. There is nothing to be said against the
Pope. Who belongs to the Virgin Mary. How else would
he know how modest and yet greedy for souls this
woman is? For instance, the woman can pout her lips like
a funnel to receive the Direktor's member when she is
kneeling. Now don't you go pretending you've never
seen it on your secret home movie screen! Just like
yourself, supposedly Jesus, that perpetual travelling
representative in Austria and related territories, went
here and there to see if there was any need to improve or
punish or affect. And in the course of his travels he met
you. Whom he loves as he loves himself. And what of
you? Do you only love the money that belongs to others?
Right. So write a letter to the paper, sounding off at
those who have no God, or, if they did have one,
wouldn't know what to do with him.

All of it belongs to us!

The woman pays no heed at all to her glottis as the car
grinds to a halt. She howls as if she'd been oiled, and in
fact she is pretty well oiled, the effects of that cheap wine

haven't worn off yet. She yawps and yaps and bawls till the night sits bolt upright in its bed and lights begin to go on all around. Including the lights in her own house. Where the ponderous person who is the manager of a paper mill climbs into his boisterous body. Doubtless rejoicing to have back what he believed to be lost. He stands at the mouth of the warm bear's cave, where all the instruments play, even at the touch of a child's fingers. Gerti, is that you, he asks, looking beyond his own limited horizons. Who on earth could wish to lose something he owns? Soon, thanks be to God, he will again be able to grab at her epicentre between her legs. To see if the bread basket's still hung high enough. Out of reach of others. Though there are more crumbs in it now. And then he'll give her a taste of his baguette in the breadroom. His trusty tool will go to work, wielded by an honest master of the craft, where none else has ever been. You'd better believe it. The Man is slow to make his choice between different deities (sport and politics) but very quick when, fore hooves first, he clumps onto the stage where all the action concerns him and his works. The young man does not hesitate to make eye contact and offer good evening. The woman, complete with dressing-gown, is tipped sideways out of the door, displaying no desire to couple once again. The young rogue, that young body now idly thinking it would like something to eat, is buried beneath her. When her husband welcomes her back, she knows that the very least he'll be wanting is to nibble her ears. Soon he'll be feeling right as rain, ready to pour down on his wife, for not only the woman but also the art that dwells within us and our hi-fis is at his beck and balls. The Direktor whispers smut, tut tut, in the woman's ear, a promise of what lies ahead, lies willingly abed. How nice to have a woman in the home again! And the boy needs his mother, too. Who shows him important things. Things he can get a far better look at on TV, mind you.

*

God appears in the form of Nature. In voices. From the outside world. Where employees live, their arms wide open, forever clasping nothingness. Their food is bloody with the wounds inflicted on the animal during its lifetime. They also eat the doughy clods they've baked, lumpy and shapeless as their own bodies or laughter. Formless as their brood, the angry inheritors, running after them like snot from an unstopped nostril. Their children! Getting on people's nerves with what they and TV call sport. From time to time a specimen of humanity falls apart. Have you ever noticed? You're sitting next to someone, some perfectly natural specimen, riding public transport of some description because neither of you can afford a car. If you did notice, nobody else did. Some of the offspring they made on the night shift won't even make shift for the factory. They are the alcoholic vapour they exhale. Not even their serious illnesses seem to upset them. Warm-hearted togetherness such as you witness here in the Direktor's home, a family circle with wife and child, the shadows of bodies cast on other bodies, darkness at noon, while others toil and sweat — all this and more you can see on the screen, to satisfy your wretched curiosity (when all you really want to see is yourself, in a different role at last, and preferably not a cardboard character). Beneath the dome of his desire, the Direktor is seen by the villagers to have space still for at least one further person, of his own choosing. All of them work in his factory. These creatures in their commuter trains, jammed into their compartments, eating their *wurst* and waiting for the worst. Now night has gently descended and condescended to join us. Now let us sleep.

The Direktor half hands his wife from the car that gave her a lift, the woman half lifts, nay elevates herself from the clammy hands of the student. Back down to earth. The young man has prospects and no need of any paper mill, so now we see the rapid-fire colt politely helping the mare back to the stall. Now it is done. He hears himself describe how he picked up the woman on a country lane, drunk. She still makes a confused and disoriented impression. Shivering with the cold. At the threshold she is ordered to pull herself together and come in. This is her kennel. Right here. Where her loved ones, loved by virtue of her work, her labour, are resting now. The moment God's looking the other way, they're pawing between each other's thighs. Don't go expecting them to leave their sex in peace. They're forever wanting to cock their little guns and fire, bang! It's theirs, all theirs. In their tales, their tails are silent beasts of prey. Even the body is not-so-silently praying to be a beast with a tail. The Direktor loads and overloads the weapon slung under his belly. The child is interested not only in art and sport but also in pop music on the radio. To be truthful, I'm not really sorry for the boy. The woman sticks fast as tar to her husband's shoulder. From within, an instrument is already probing the trousercloth and wanting to go home to its hole. This woman is unlike the others, who are lucky if they can find jobs as domestics, since there are no longer jobs in the factory to afford an alternative existence to generating living things. Women are forever being picked, sledgehammered, drilled, forever worked at in the mine, all mine. Or the slags are tossed where they belong, on the slag heap. To bring forth children. Ever noticed that at night it's only the wealthy that enter the commonwealth of pleasure, never the common folk? That's when the rich do their work! Let's face it, they have to work some time or other, since the poor beggars do exist, when all's said and undone, with their Mercedes and their birthright to conquest.

The undressing-gown flaps about the woman. She's dead tired. The alcohol heat inside her has subsided. What's the point of all this noise the Direktor's making now? Why has this immodestly-clad woman returned to

Nature's cave of games? Dogs don't go around off the leash! She coughs when the Man smites her on the shoulders and the conscience. His worries carry the day and he crushes his wife to his heart, wraps himself about her, we won't be needing this dressing-gown any more. If only that young fellow would be off. Who makes possible a comparison of the body in its present state and its original condition as approved by the planning authorities. Patience. In good time we'll all have the pleasure of casting off our mis-shapen outer self.

The original version of this paper mill manager looked better, too, than we in our cruel inhumanity can now imagine. This woman loves. And is not loved. In this she is not unique. Fate is as inevitable as this finger I'm pointing at you now. The woman is less than nothing at all now. The young man laughs at the gratitude of the Direktor, who's had his doggie returned to him. The disrespectful youngster reads the expression of the man who considers himself his rival. But he wouldn't mind a paper mill. Instead of having to toil over law and jurisprudence. He cannot feel the equal of the people who slouch to the factory, bliss in their eyes, for they are to see the one who has given work to one and all. And what is the student thinking of? Who he's playing tennis with tomorrow.

The Herr Direktor talks and talks, the flames of speech flicker, the tongues of fire lick, he's warming up. There the womenfolk sit, simmering, wearing naughty lingerie and provoking their menfolk so that their motors rev high and they want to burn up the highway. It is not on them but on the poor that the world heaps its wrath. The poor go walking along the banks with their children, where chemicals corrode the waters. The main thing is to have a job at all. And to come home from work with a suitable industrial disease.

*

Like a heavy unhooked door, Gerti sinks back into her husband's hinges. The question is, will she hold when the tempests of time bring storms and snows? She wants the young man to take another swig of her, preferably tomorrow. Right now, though, another man, a regular, is going to be messing with her fuses till the lights go out. The Direktor knows that this woman shall rest in that place only which has been ordained her lawful wedded grave. So that he can appreciate her best sides (left and right). This creature is his, belongs to him. To serve his regular needs, like a jar to pee in. Anything imagination can dream up can indeed be done with a living, lively member that distends and then shrinks again, the only question is: whose? Love opens the woman's eyes. Like knocking at the natural landscape, you rap with your rod and wait to see if water's flowing from the rock. The work goes quickly, but are the workers happy? No.

And the boy blubs, boo hoo, because he can't get to sleep. Not if mummy doesn't tell him how to wipe his feet clean of life. Mummy mummy, comes his whine from inside, and a malicious little head appears, the fruit of her womb complete with worm. It would be better if the child were asleep now so that he wouldn't have to witness anything. His dough has been kneaded long enough, now he can rise, arise and go. And early in the morning the weary people arise and go, free of the burden of beauty. They wander like deer. Now the child is there. Tomorrow morning it will be smeared as full of jam as Mother is with Father's slime. And the Holy Ghost's. Their son dashes in. Having missed his mum. Father shuts the door in the student's face, he wants to spread his wife's thighs at his leisure and take a look if anyone's been grazing in his meadow, where his sacred cow's at pasture. Mother crosses no-man's-land to her child. Welcome! The Direktor wants his wife to be a part of him as summer is a part of the year. All that's needed is for day to waken too. The child has a title to proper care. Who doesn't long hourly for that sneak-thief, Love? And I bet you have a cuddly lamb too. Now who's been missing whom? This mountain is here for only one reason: to put an end to this vale of tears, so that production and viewing will peak again. The snow is pale. The Man sets great store by good works, works where paper is made for the well-being of us all. Let me write it down, quite un-ambiguously: paper could cut me open as a paper knife slits paper. I'd like to meet the person who could make a new woman of me out of the things I say.

But what more do we want than to get our wages in the pocket of our failure. That is: no doubt we do want to become something, no doubt we do want to be a little more, at least on paper. And we want our feelings too, as we sit there at home, through our own fault, through our own most grievous fault, with none to keep us company but the phone.

He's heartless, this man. Like fire he consumes the house. He drags his wife around. The child starts to shout. Outside, a solitary exhaust struggles to attract the attention of sleepers who, like animals, register the tempest as it rages but don't dare say anything. Not even during the daytime can they join in the muscular games of the beautiful, wealthy flesh. Their pleasures are burdened with oppressions, society needs the poor, q.e.d. The young man drives off. And no sooner has he quit the shunting cunting yard where they linked their couplings than the woman pounds on the door which her longing long since smashed through the wall with the axe of desire. Eyeless, she stares into nowhere, any-where, wherever she might see him again. But men are such creatures of violence, regardless they set fire to their houses where their families lie asleep, ignorant of what the figures in the bank statements mean. Let's get undressed and look at these other figures instead, deceive someone with our genitals. Truly, men cover all the highways and byways with themselves. But you don't care, not you, that a human being is suffering wrongings and longings before your very eyeways.

Longing is a stick that this woman has fetched herself, fetch! She needs the excitement. For her house is in order and delivered too. So she quests abroad. And then she thinks continually of what she has found. And tips it like a packet soup into her turbulent bubbling boiling waters and stirs it round and stirs a stranger's heart. After all, the Catholic Congress needs its far-off Pope as well. Who journeys to join us, though when he is here in our fatherland, lo! he's suddenly just another human being like you and me, don't I know him from somewhere. For him, everyone comes last, a loser, last past the post. Not so with love. Men at least can get somewhere, they can thumb a lift, but women are always wanting a lift from their feelings, a high, and being let down. The whole human race is in a ferment of wishes, forever wondering what to buy.

Where have you been? The words batter Gerti, Father's blows strike the boy as well, his kith and kin, who claws tight hold of Mother. Let's not bother describing this Laocoön group, the three of them in each other's toils, holding tight, down they go.

The Man's rage is huge. Moil and toil and turmoil, he's coming to the boil, time to cool the heat with a jet of foam. He wants the woman to take off her clothes right away. So that she measures up to his size. He wants to conduct his lightning into her. Not that his wildfire could ever be tamed by her, and anyway he has plenty of matches. To create himself anew, as often as need be. To have the woman bake his baguette, cook his meat, pickle his gherkin, and eat. The child is put to bed with a glass of fruit juice, quiet now! Leave the woman to Father. Don't go yapping and barking at her and jumping and frisking

and grabbing. Mother's back, that's enough. And Father's
bird is already chirping over her furrow. The Man drags
her into the bedroom to force entry into her and piss on
her. Good to have her home! The cow cud have been
dead, cunt she?

The Direktor stands like a glowing cigarette butt by the
hay of his bed and tosses himself away. Fear flares up in a
blaze: holy night, a holy roll in the Austrian hay, where
tales are told of the holy animal come to eat at the haybox
of social welfare. It's not long since Christmas, now it's
already practically time for springtime wishes. There
goes Father, from one to the other, in all the majesty of
his calling and becking. The woman wishes she were
gone, she knows what youth is and she knows what she
has lost and that time spent here now is time lost. That's
how it goes, when you've played with life and lost! Now
someone else's tongue is jammed down the woman's
throat, take a good hard pull to wash away the taste.
From the top of his ski-jump the Man swoops down on
the woman. She covers her face with shadows, and yet
what is hers is torn from her, no power on earth would
be equal to the Direktor's hefty sex. He only needs to
believe, like the whole national skiing team! Yet for the
woman it is as if he had been as completely cleared out of
her life as the prominent people of today whose names
will merely sound silly in ten years' time. The woman
wants nothing but youth. She would shoot young
beautiful bodies on fast film in the hope of getting a shot
at them, fast, wait and see what develops. These visions
seem heaven-sent. Meanwhile her arms are pulled from
her face and Father descends upon her, leaving her
cheeks red with wining and whining. What people live
on, apart from their hopes, is a mystery to me. They
seem to invest everything in cameras and hi-fis. There's
no room in their houses for life any more. Once the act of
purchasing is accomplished, everything is really over,
though in fact nothing is over, or else it wouldn't be

there any more. After all, burglars want their share of
the fun as well.

The Man waits till his water's come to the boil. Then he
tosses his wife in after first removing her dressing-
gown. His signal is up, the track's clear, here comes the
express. He doesn't need any egging on from her, he has
two eggs anyway down there with his sausage, quite
enough for two. It is as if his prick were out of its mind
with the thought that someone else might have gone
grubbing in her cunt, driving his truck in and mucking
her up. His anger wears the Man out before his time: too
much energy is wasted on shouting, till the very vaults of
heaven are echoing. Outside, everything has been over-
powered by ice and snow. Nature does generally get
things right, but now and then you have to lend a helping
hand so she can enjoy her meal at our table in peace and
quiet. The rain bursts from the Man, into the woman.
the two little rugs of her dugs are given a good beating
out. The two kilos of his stock and barrel hang down like
rocks. Fearlessly he scatters his gravel on the woman, so
he can go for a walk in her with a firm grip underfoot.

The boy has got up again, sleepy, he'd best not rattle at
the bathroom door like that or he'll be tipped out with
the bathwater. The Man forces the woman's head right
back to prevent her from yelling. His bird is wide awake,
it's locked in the cage of her mouth, which is where it
likes to be, flapping about till the woman starts to retch
and heave and her vomit travels along his shaft and
dribbles down his dangling testicles. Too bad. His glans is
yanked out of her pharynx and the woman tipped
halfway over the tub. His prick is stiff as a bull-rush, and
now he rushes her like a bull and tucks his prick up in bed
where it belongs, he tolls the bells of her breasts, alcohol
gushes from her like water, and potent drops of the good
stuff squirt into her cunt. No, the Direktor won't allow
this woman simply to tumble out of his nest. What does

she think she's doing, obeying her own senses, not him?
Man and wife are one flesh.

The woman only appeared for a minute or so in the arena
where consumers learn to swim. Now she is sitting in a
filled bath, getting a soaping. The dressing-gown, long
since crumpled, will have to be cleaned, trimmed and
ironed. The Man tears whole handfuls of hair from her
pussy as she goes about her washing and refurbishing.
He digs into the gills of her privates and his soapy fingers
invade her ground water where he shot his wad. She
thrashes and whimpers, it stings! Out front her coveted
fruits hang plump on their branches. The Direktor
makes an investigative grab at the tips of the sausage
skins which someone else has left, he twirls them round
three fingers and then slowly releases them. Hard as
buttons, the areolas' cold eyes stare at us. You can never
do anything right for the lordsandmasters, not even if
you were a queen. And already the terrible vessels that
must receive the contents of the men are clattering. With
a whiffle and sniffle the waiting-room doors swing shut
on the boneyards of the unemployed. We shall find a way
to tame those floods as well.

10

THEY MIGHT REST IN PEACE and security. But first the sunshine that peeps through the forks of their limbs would needs cast its piercing light upon them: there is something they can do that it's worth having a body for! They can doff each other's hats. With a few thrusts they work their way through to the other side of each other. Their dwelling place seems a very heaven. And before they (like the cheetah) have taken the few mighty bounds that will take them to the drinking trough of the mighty, they'll have coupled several times over. Like motes of dust in a sunbeam. Why else would they have and hold each other, care for each other with water and showers of emotion, as if they were to be canonized? Every part of their bodies has earned their partner's attention and love. Like the farmers who work on the side and get on the foreman's nerves by forever falling asleep on the job. Laying into the animals, slitting their throats, nodding and winking at blind horses: all the tricks that have been performed on themselves, dozens of times. Here comes the small farmer from the stalls and sheds, in wellingtons, because his good shoes are at home together with his good wife. The blood of the rabbit the children loved is dripping from the sleeve of his jacket. But even this man, who is on this earth to have a life, has an occasional friendly side when he drags a girl off the dance floor into the bushes. And she scarcely notices what she's putting up her resistance to.

But those who dwell in the light that enters through their blinds experience things altogether differently. They are at their best for each other. Even when they oil the silent ointment of time upon their bodies. You hardly see it, time, that suntan lotion of creation, but those who have anointed themselves with it are safe from the rays and noise. Look at this woman, for instance, in this photograph. Time seems to have passed her by without leaving any trace at all. There she is, in her locker, where her husband has stored her for safe keeping.

The big kids who attend the school of profit are filled with worries about nationalization, which tugs at our purse strings as this Direktor tugs at his wife's dugs. The owners have given him to understand that the big companies, wonderful in their greed as in their wrath, would like to play for mortal stakes with the people of the country. The children of those who lose out are the first to realize what side their bread is buttered: no matter how thin the slice, you need to earn your daily bread and save it up in your bank account. On target for the super premium. And maybe the Direktor will play along and sing a chorus too, hallelujah.

He has other worries, then, which he wears with a ruffled air. He wears his hair parted, unruffled, and his genitals in a bag he's brought for his wife. How her eyes will light up! Wait and see! His high monthly income brings indelible joy and cheer upon his weary but notably solvent head. We servants, though, are known for what we are. For there is life in the depths. The people flock to the pub. Soon we shall have all our sheep safely in from the rain and cold, we'll be feathering our own nest, doing our business. Our rapid growth causes suffering to the nobodies who can't see further than the ends of their noses and yet travel further than that, bare-headed and full of resolve, and still end up in front of the boss. Who says he can't comply with their wishes, and swish! — their wishes are scythed down in swathes by the company's resolution to rationalize (ah, these rational people). Truly, the Direktor is in his element. He takes the measure of others, for he is immeasurably wealthy in the eyes of the people who learn how to fall like autumn leaves beside him. Softly, so that they don't disturb him when he plays the violin. He can see no reason why he should restrain himself inside his belt, which looks good on him, for perhaps another has dwelt inside his wife, where only he should dwell. My thanks for listening to these insults.

Tenderly, every inch the jovial deity he can sometimes be when he's in the mood for his wife, he leans over her skin, which is musky with animal vapour. She wants to sleep now. Not a well-advised wish. She is full of her recent past, and if we get real close we'll notice it too: the future is wide open to the young, if they have studied and their parents have learned to play them off against one another. Let the neighbours' children rot like fallen fruit where they lie. And this woman is already wide open to a hopeless love, cosy as a rabbit hutch the day after the battle, she has already shlepped in all her furniture and there's flowery wallpaper too! From her pussy only a narrow path leads on, and there he stands, the student, together with all my readers, an educated youngster, mild of temper and tempest, waiting to get in again. If we all keep together and keep everything we've got together, our premonitions may come true. We are unnecessary! If we have any title to live at all, then in the memory of some loved animal we have fed or some loved person we have fed ourselves to.

The Direktor could batter his wife, bat her skull-first into the garden any time he chooses, she'd better watch out if she goes batting her eyelids again. But he doesn't bother just now because his urges are gathering like waters in a woodland spring. Useless tears will make her mascara run, she'll be masked, unrecognizable. Patches of purple will blossom on the moorland of her body. Poverty isn't the only way to beat people into submission when day inflames the early hours and coffee gushes into people's gobs. It is not good if we women have nothing to love but the cleaning of rooms and are not subjected to daily inspection to see if our organs are all in order. Don't worry. We're all just as we were. Just the same. Soon the abyss will be full of us. Our detached houses will be o'ershadowed by the interest on the loan. And the boss will be off to the byre, to us animals on the chains of our wishes, waiting to be kicked about. Anyone with a smallholding and a little house of his own will be the first to taste the bitterness of unemployment: so say the people who have just been shopping at a divine little boutique and then squeeze in behind their desks where no one can soothe them any more. Not even the ever so slight friction of water on the sex brushes they use to paint each other's wishes can make them good to the goods and chattels they keep chattering with fear in the death cell. Often it's a drive of several hours till they're home with their human partners and can switch on the current that zaps through the chairs.

You don't go eating out if you've built a beautiful house of your own. Shadow falls on the street. Workers returning home want to turn in somewhere for a beer. The Direktor's brow is innocent of effort. As a violinist he is just a fart in a hurricane, but he can still service his wife in just five minutes. His suspension is good, look at him banging his little jug at her udder, did you see how he stuck it in her mouth? He's still having problems parking those wings. But the lordsandmasters always like shooting the rapids, getting their business done, they're always in a hurry. And your cunt'd be on fire too if someone took a slash in it every day! Outside a zealous policeman passes, making notes. There's many a one of you has seen a strong man weaken at the knee to see a no-hunting sign, but when it comes to the women back home where it's warm and dry, the season's always open and the game is waiting for the hunter. To come and play. This lordandmaster, in whom a need for excitement is stirring, appears like a sign in the heavens above the woman. His tongue sets a pulse beating in the can of juice she has jammed between her thighs. You mustn't be wary of brandishing the fist you thump on the table. Elsewhere, people are seeing to their backfiring exhausts and brooding over their engines, so that they won't be late for work. But in the evening they flare up like flames if their wives' cooking isn't any good. What's this, they say, and the wife casts her gaze up as if she had just climbed the Alps. These people don't have much time left to languish after a beautiful object of their desire with breasts up front (no point having them elsewhere). Even our cars use up our last bit of juice.

The Direktor clings to the woman who shares the bed. She's been worn out and knocked about so long, perhaps he's intending to finish her off. Let's take a look. She really mustn't go prowling about to see if someone will be a real man for her and stick his tongue in her pussy.

The Direktor uses no contraceptives because what he'd like best would be to see a whole lot more miniatures of himself. Only small ones, mind, he won't be put in the shade by anyone. He steps out onto the path of light and cracks open the woman's mouth with his drill. His grip starts her coughing, a shudder passes through her from rudder to udder. The Man seems fascinated by the fact that he can give birth to the entire length of his dong single-handed. He is changed. He quarrels with the woman on account of his slow-burning stove. What an active substance it must be, blessed trinity, growing to three times its single size without divine intervention! No martyrdom required! What a man! And then he rains down on his nearest and dearest. Elsewhere they have steps leading up to the houses, though no one wants to live in them, given the choice. The poorest of the poor find themselves at last, with their small steps.

Yelling, the Herr Direktor drills his way into Gerti's

mouth. First he has to be beside himself if he wants to get inside her, these aren't the times to have a little something on the side, and the Direktor was always encouraged as a youngster to show his good side. Put up a good show, fight the good fight, and always make sure your instrument's tuned. His son already plays an instrument too. The slopes tip whole handfuls of acid trees down the mountainside. The woman kicks and is kicked. Till she screams. No, this isn't the time for wandering about the house or smoking a cigarette or boozing or behaving in an angry, threatening way to the staff. Her nightie is stripped off so that she can be groped from various sides, yes, the Direktor is a many-sided talent, right! We often use the bed. It is where we sleep off the war of the sexes. To think we could simply inspect the ranks ad infinitum there and work our way up to mediocrity. In no other field do you rise so fast, always supposing (in the case of women) that the face you have suits you. The crag, after all, doesn't go to the pasture; the animals go to it, to rub their heads on it. Now the woman is flailing and thrashing as if she were out for immortality there amid her electrical appliances. She fades away like the dying echo of a cry, the cry you give when in broad daylight the lightning, that incorrigible flasher, can't control itself and zaps into the TV set. The set, entertainment for the dark night of the soul, will have to be repaired. The Direktor wants to fire his gun again today. To be sure of his wife — lying there bleeding, breathing, retching. Sleep heavy in her eyes. Bile rising in her gorge as this intruder rises in her gorge.

Of course he can spread her cheeks any time he likes with those great heavy paws of his! Those buttocks are his property, just as God is ours. Her sphincter squeaks like an old shoe. In less than five minutes he'll have shot his bolt again. Keep clear at all times! For this Man can't stand life alone, and others have to stand him every day. The woman's body is at his service most of the time,

every now and then it seems as if the sun is going to
shine. Get these people out of the way, the farmer's left
the furrow ever so slightly ajar! I left them sated and
sated I find them, and no lamp lights the way in this
terrain. So they plough and rape their wives, and bow
and scrape to the works committees, not that the
committees have any real power left. Sometimes before
you can say Jack Robinson a new skilled worker has been
given a dressing down and is waiting in the workshop to
be dressed and salted. His field is limited to the very end.
There are few women seated at breakfast, which is
served by the housekeeper. Opposite the man. With
sunglasses shading their drawn worn forlorn eyes. One
place exactly is occupied by them. At night they were
ridden and rocked like the heavenly horses children learn
to ride on. But the children sit more securely in the
saddle! This Man takes as many liberties as our
president, he is almost as great a burden for us
wanderers to bear upon our shoulders. He says that
Mozart was a wonderful composer. He too enjoys
playing. But on a smaller scale, if you compare the frame.
With a little space left over for hobbies. At the Salzburg
Festival he has an opportunity to test his stamina. Father
agrees with himself. Giving a merry wink, he penetrates
his wife's sphincter. She restrains the cry that's straining
at the leash, after all, she's a married woman now.
Nobody learns to read without paying for it.

The Direktor dips a toe in her cool waters and then
emerges from the gloom into the sunshine. In every
respect he is at ease in the mansion of himself. He may as
well be silent. You can live in a house like snow on the
grass of course, but you can keep your chained-up
member so busy that the clinking and jingling never
stops. There are many women but only one Man. He
bends over the woman's hind legs and whispers of the
erotic kicks he could get in the brothel any time, instead
of which he puts up with her kicks. Erotic! The word was

coined for the Erikas of this world, not the Gertis. It is what gives this solemn ceremony its meaning. The Man has to bear the animal within in mind, and what does the animal do when it's been bared? Guess. A conversation with the world and its well-oiled machine parts. In an ante-room where they wait till the women come to their assistance with the musty holes knocked open by the hail. The life's work of some of them will be completely forgotten by the earth. Reliably, though, the Man discovers his ejaculated semen below him, and wallows in the certainty that his child will live on after him, to torment others in his stead. Let's turn a blind eye to it all. Who lays everything waste and nonetheless is always wanting to start afresh? Right. He buys new clothing for the child, and Mother, since Nature has its limits, has to wash it. They show mothers doing so on TV. This mother plays piano, as far as the pedals will take her.

The Direktor has fucked his wife's tube enough, now he gapes at an empty screen. Takes a look at himself. And, an amiable stranger inclined over the engine now that it's idle, he fiddles with his pet. As you might stroke a dog. He dribbles saliva on her, 'scuse me. Your home territory isn't where some other man has been before you. For the Man, the woman is a constant factor/ factotum because she keeps her feet on the ground while he aims straight at the heart and writes computer programmes by way of a hobby. That'll leave them speechless. Light shines upon the field. Tomorrow Gerti is sure to be still there. He doesn't want any other man hanging round when she's hanging loose, boring into her when she's bored. Now the Direktor appears from out of his blind corner, works his way into place like the stream pouring into the valley. That's how he'd like it. Formula One impatiently pawing at the starting line. And all around the selfsame night can never cleanse the poor of themselves. Quite the contrary: they're cold, and they have to warm up at their wives' pussies. They don't want to be too late tomorrow, at the factory, our greatest good, where they are not so much wanted as expected. If they are in flight, they are fetched down. Many of them have to saw frost-damaged branches off their fruit trees. The Direktor gobs terrible wads of filth in his wife's ear. She might simply be forgotten, like a rucksackful of rancid sandwiches, it's up to her. Any time at all! She can have the good life, just as long as she doesn't go overcrowding her knickers. Just as long as the way inside is kept clear and gritted, so that the Man knows where to go if he's disaffected. Got to slam the ball home, goal! And what of her? He yanks her hair as if he were still steering. Nearing the end, his trembling member crashes into her undergrowth. The Man punches the nape of her neck and the voice in which he addresses her is awesome. Could it be that this woman is thinking of another, better-loved poker? Could it be possible? So it happens that the Direktor's brimful cup passes her by and its contents are deposited on her skin, a heap of refused refuse. This woman is unworthy that the Direktor should incline towards her at an angle of 45 degrees. Let us now drink two quarters, no, three quarters of our fill! At one time the jolly conquerors didn't have so many interruptions to contend with in their conquests. But now there blows a sharper wind.

The people of the country will soon have to rise and shine, harried from one place to another, even before they know where they're at. But wait a moment. Even they enjoy an advantage: springtime will be theirs as well, with its puffing and blowing and zephyrs and fresh air. But in the mean time we shall have achieved far more. Because *we* shall have forged ahead. We are confident, we go to the theatre or a concert or exhibition where we recognize our own image, cast by nothing but the light of *their* wretched eyes. Yes, we are on the list! If you take a look down there, you'll see a wild heap of unemployed believers at the mercy of the banks, you wouldn't credit it. The light in those eyes, ah, at the end of the federal highway, has gilded nothing but factory dividends. But they forgot to indicate, and, misjudging the bend, dazzled by the glare of a job at long last, plunged into the river. One really shouldn't go falling asleep at the wheel early in the morning. And what is becoming of the taxes we pay in the mean time? The money is squandered like people, wasted like lives, an expensive sports car in a slim and talented country, see, where industry takes a sharp bend downhill. Of course people are run over elsewhere too. Now let us continue on our restless way, leaving barely detectible tracks on the federal tarmac and to our children a colour TV set and a video recorder per head.

11

THEN AT BREAKFAST THEY just can't get enough. The child comes racing down and bounds about before Father, what a young rascal. Little sunshine, he is. Worth his weight in gold. Father wants his son to be a plucky fellow, not a yellow fucker. But it's not plucky the kid is, it's lucky, pushing his luck, always out for the lucky dip at the joke shop in town, always wanting something bought. Me me me. He'll scarcely heed his mates in the distance. They have to watch as the Direktor's son runs out of money (just as they run out of time, time to knock at the door of the business world, which is ajar, neither open to them nor closed). At the Volksschule the son sits in class with kids from poor homes, which is logical enough from an educational point of view, but it's war out there in those cottages! Some of these sons and daughters reek of the byre from their long morning's work with the cattle, up to their ankles in leaden shit. There they all are, the bodies, huddled together, till lack of money sweeps them off to the factories. Never seen flowers like these blowing and fading in the factories? Off the child mischievously skips across the field, upsetting the precarious balance of Nature and natural law. (And the child's quite right to hammer a mole with a stick or whish downhill on skis. But then, you're right too, gentle reader, off for a healthy walk, wrapped up in a genuine, natural cloud of pure new wool.) From time to time a gun is fired into the guts of the forest. Cesspits are meant to protect Nature from human kind and its waste, but who will protect humanity from bank employees who get up early just to look up at the Alps? During the night, thank God, there's been a slight thaw, which keeps would-be skiers in suspense well before they're suspended from the lift. Round the bases of trees, ice is packed like the moulded polystyrene used to pack those delicate hi-tech gadgets that make our eyes pop out.

Some would see it quite differently, mind. Here comes the housekeeper with her shopping trolley. The ground, still frozen in places, drones under the wheels as if it were hollow. As well as above us, there must be something below us, too. Have you put your affairs in order, are you having an affair, do you have a fair weather friend? No? Well, just wait till there's a knock at *your* door. Who knows, maybe one of these slimmed-down well-built jobless fellows out to sell you a magazine subscription. So that you understand the arts and the economy and politics the better.

Being a man, the Direktor can look down on his wife, since she's sitting down there in her usual place where the light from the window cannot fall upon her. Falling upon her is the prerogative of her husband. It is still dark. Gerti is wearing sunglasses. The boy, agog from the TV, comes romping in squawking with greed for another new thing that this time just has to be bought, to take him out of this good old world fast gadgets and the clothes to go with them, so he will walk in happiness for all of his days. For he wants to go off out with the tide, the boy does. His father, from the dark and mighty planet that is his head, utters a word of command. His choice has fallen upon this morning as the right time to fall upon the mother of this child once again. Improving on his nocturnal performance, he has forced himself upon her, just for a short while, short being the operative word. Just as one sits in an armchair, absorbed for a brief moment only in the contrived honesty of the evening news, the Direktor has settled heavily into her, letting himself drop, docking his nozzle from behind at his favourite pump where he tanks up with the consolations and sacraments of life. If only a man could really work this pump to his heart's content! Super! His words force a way into her ear; he wants to go over her accounts of yesterday's misdemeanour again, he's her master book-keeper. Genuine grass will hopefully make an appearance some time or other, now that we've been sowing the fake seed at scrap car lots and service areas, where even a rubber needs a thorough warming before it's unpeeled. We are so orderly and so spendthrift, spending ourselves, casting our seed upon stony ground and then keeping the fact from our human partners, keeping it to ourselves so that the pleasure's ours alone. His wife's thighs are for him only, the Direktor, the terrible visitant. They roast in the hot oil of his lust. He deep-fries. Busily he unloads on her ramp, palpitating, and some time he'll bring her a present of a brooch or a steel bracelet. And it's over. We're free again. Home. Where we belong. But richer than before, when we laughed at the neighbour. You have an open invitation to come and take a look! Don't worry, nothing will happen when the gentleman with the fizz and bezazz comes knocking at your door to jazz you up and pop your cork! Quite the contrary: a woman's expected to be delighted! Next thing you know he'll be packaging himself up in a box! The blue heavens have serious intentions where the landscape is concerned. Business is flourishing.

This woman will doubtless be off at the drop of a hat to the hairdresser's, to have herself trimmed for Michael. Brimful of love, the parents clash above the son. Who is immersed in his playthings just as Father is immersed in Mother. Engrossed; it's gross. The manchild alone with his toy. Fetch that child, now. At one time blades of grass grew here, now the knife-blade's at the heart: who could stay calmly on his own pathway and merely look on? They all have to make a song and dance of their sufferings, piss out something creative so that everyone will notice and love them. Everyone asks the son in what way he is superior to the other kids. It's enough to make Mother's breasts squirt milk: the boy just doesn't seem to possess an immortal soul. At least, he gives his mother no joy. Already he wants to be off skiing again, off with the others being taken for a ride on the lifts. Let's hope

they don't dare too much and have an accident! Now the
mother greedily kisses her child, who twists free of her
grip. Benevolently Father paws at the carpet, wishing he
were alone with his wife once again to paw her.
Sometimes when the child's attention is distracted he
shoves a finger or two into the most exciting part of her,
that slit, which he finds so enticing that he buys her
expensive things to wear so that she can cover it up.
Secretly he sniffs his hand. It's a winning hand, as
winning as he is, as relentless as the light. Meanwhile,
Mother lavishes kisses on him, loving the boy and
spoiling him rotten, lavishing toys and junk on him as if
they were lovers. Father thumps the table goodnaturedly.
He has already made use of the woman today; presumably
a child has uses for a mother too. Still, it doesn't do to
overdo these things! His son needs to learn a little
moderation and modesty, it'll come in handy when he
loans his nice new skis to those of more modest means,
for a moderate sum, so that he can stuff yet more
surprises into his mouth at the sweetshop. The boy is a
lazy little local railway. Already he has a flourishing
trade going with his various equipment, bearing happiness even to the most oafish ignoramuses (the kind of
characters who imagine that roller-skating can help in
the quest for a loophole in the system, when everyone
knows the Alps are in the way). All these kids know is
that it must cost a fair bit to have racing skis. This man
and this heavenly woman — how alive they feel when
they touch each other up! Their eyes are fixed on each
other's as if nails had been driven in.

Father the fiddler, pardon me, the violin-player, would
doubtless praise his son for working such fiddles. Let
him be an example to you, you who administer the snow
in this community, even demanding money for the use of
this flaky white sporty stuff. There it lies, on the fields of
home. And there you go, one of the numberless slaves of
sport, wearing the brightly coloured overalls that you

sport everywhere you go, whether it's the ski slope or the disco. It's all one. And you're number one. But first you have to be hauled up high, to be close to God, where time is valued more highly than your downhill time recorded with a stop-watch by your lady wife who has come along on foot. Suddenly life is a more familiar thing to you when you're at the snowy brink holding a gadget to your guaranteed-to-wash-out body. The poor can't hold back the waters, they freeze beneath them; all they can do is cautiously step across, with the exalted majesty of the mountains above them, from where no help will ever come, we regret to say, yours faithfully etc. Here they all are, a colourful multitude scattered from their offices, nicely dressed, rejoicing in the taverns, bent over their skis as if over someone they loved, sliding and whooshing right on down, well, that's it, what else did you expect them to do on skis? And then they get together, full of good cheer like a care packet, bundles of fun on the air waves, live from the village inn where an Alpine band is playing, say, and the poor look on and have no idea what's going on or how it is that these stars of the TV screen are there before their very eyes, blown in by a wanton wind.

Coffee is administered to Mother by the housekeeper. It's not as if she didn't have an unopened bottle hidden away in the wardrobe, mind. It'd be better if the children's group weren't coming today to blow their trumpets. Oh no, they're not coming till tomorrow. To rehearse their song and dance and claptrap for the firefighters' ball. On holidays, various things gather on the turntable, the daily round, and turn out to be the St Matthew Passion or some other tune that pleaseth our ears. Horrified, the woman stares at her hands, which she does not recognize. Language draws itself up erect before her like her husband's penis, you rattle the chain and whoosh off you go downhill. On her day off she's been overwhelmed by a feeling, a sense of the white

radiance of Nature, if that's what it really was, mere
Nature. Let's all try to look our best and get to know
someone and be there just for him to see and no one else.
That young man who crossed her terrain in a brief half
hour: is he still thinking of her at all? He stepped in the
heap she deposited. It's well worth being special, dis-
tinctive. The woman's going to ponder life as someone
else's goddess. Perhaps we should go along to the
hairdresser's too? Afterwards we could take a look at the
mangy workers in the workaday Christmas manger.

In passing, the Direktor gropes deep in the woman's
cleavage, where the most important parts of her general
appearance are visible. That's right, that's how pictures
are supposed to be. This woman won't be going anywhere. She has something to do: take a look at his tail and
lick it and insert it into herself. She mustn't be seduced
by some character off the street. The countryside is dully
aglow, but those who might see it see nothing because
their miserable shadows are colliding with those of the
jolly sporting crowd, hugging themselves tight to glide
more slippily down the wind. Elsewhere, in places where
the unstoppable tourist trade hasn't produced such
liveliness and laughter, things are not managed quite so
amenably, I fear. In grubby kitchens, cold fire crackles in
the eyes of men who have to go to work at five a.m. The
leaden sausage lies plumb in their guts, forgotten. Their
wives burst loudly into reality, demanding work instead
of children. (The children, for their part, can visit the
scale-model city at Hadersdorf, Vienna, where the
houses are tiny enough to play with and you learn to
know your place.) Everyone wants to earn a little extra,
so that they too can whoosh away on skis like a fury,
come the holidays. After work, that zestful freshness
they've achieved by using the right soap is long gone.
And, in any case, no one gets anywhere in the paper
mill's grey, oppressive halls: all there is up ahead is
figures endlessly waiting to be writ down on paper. In

the club of the powerful, the Direktor has agreed to give women preferential treatment when it comes to dismissals, i.e. he'll sack them first, to ease the burden on the men when they're at work, at least. And so that the men will have a pretext to give vent to their feelings when the foreman happens to come by.

Undisturbed, the workers watch each other in the canteen. In the light, they sing like songbirds, singing for sheer life and to make the Direktor happy. Where does it all make sense? In their sensuous wives, in whom life has expressed itself completely.

The Direktor needs his own wife. To each his own; isn't that right? The light of day has already put in an appearance and the shops are opening, though many of the people remain closed. The Man regards his wife, who is nervously waging war over a hairdresser's appointment. He watches her from the side where (as he just noticed) her breasts make a sagging impression. In his memory they are alive, as if he had created and formed them like his own child. At all events — heavens, where is my sting — it will be possible to knead the woman once more. And she belongs to him, she belongs to him: behold how bounteous, the earth and all her fruits! After school, the boy will whizz down a divine mountainside faster than you can catch your breath, you'll be bowled over by the boy (who's inherited everything from his father) or at the very least he'll overtake you. The little creature's spoilt, tagged to Mother's apron strings and thinking it will be like that for ever. But the woman wants to buy youth, she wants to find a new store that stocks it, hence too the new hairdo. To be seen, and to pass by. To pass by that man's house. That man who fed the wild animal in her yesterday. Come to think of it, hasn't she seen other young men before, standing around in bars? Standing still or in motion, they're so lovely, before they too fade from this earth. They're

busy, they've got a lot to see to before the skiing
weekend, when they'll carry on with their girlfriends,
girlfriends who take your breath away, four-colour
prints on the skin-deep glossy surface of life, and yet
make such a deep impression on your mind. If you ask
me, postcards treat landscape more sparingly than time
treats women. The scenery, taking a day off, lies tranquil
and restful in the picture you buy at the tobacconist's and
promptly scrawl full. But time simply goes too far! Like a
tempest it digs its trenches in the war-torn features of a
woman's ravaged face. Oh no, she'll say, putting a
horrified hand over her gleaming mirror image: this is
going to need some work. Not just the hairdo, which can
vary at various times. Such toil, for a mere variation on a
theme, a little night music. Her image breaks free of the
mirror's confines and goes a-roving, like her thoughts.
She knows where he lives. There he awaits her, the
skier, with price tags still attached. We're all of us
waiting. For our sack to fill up, that wage packet of the
senses, where clouds scurry on by. On the whole it's
cloudy in those parts. Let's think how to make ourselves
look good, let us think upon increase, for which of us by
taking thought cannot add just a little something?

The woman is waiting for her husband to set off for the
office as per usual. The man is waiting for a chance to get
into this wife's crevice again before he puts her on ice for
the day. The poor workers have long since been carried
off on the avalanche, bags slung over their shoulders.
Rest a while! The bus has gone. The child has been
transported away; joy-boy will be feeling superior to his
fellow-pupils. His life lines have been neatly disentan-
gled, probably by fate, the boy's constant and skilful
companion on the slopes, together with whom he's
already visited numerous foreign cities. Things have
been going well with him ever since he realized his cradle
was in a well-to-do house. The other pupils indulge

themselves with icecream, which they spin out ad infinitum. Light shines upon this mighty house. It is as if the light were waxing and waning on the waxed parquet floor and polished wainscot. Today the sun's out, just for once: so say I. The woman wants to be off to town, to a boutique, as soon as she can, in order to look nice. Why can the young man not be satisfied with her as his day-long sport? Why must he be off skiing the slopes where they're at their most virgin? Why does he always have to be the one who got there first? Except for last year, when another young fellow with all his male and female friends were having a ball there already. All the woman can think of is what she's going to wear in order to get further ahead, faster, higher. As far as her feelings will carry her. Now let's pack them away again. Her husband cannot assuage her; off he goes now to the factory. To be fair (and, after all, he's one of those who run the fair), he is about 80% responsible for her fortune and happiness. He veritably steeps her in it. Why not call in on us some time when you're in pensive mood after your travels and want to sow a whirlwind in the eyes of a fellow-being? Just come on in and ask us to help ourselves and enjoy you!

To have a well-padded vantage point, a box of her own from which to command a royal view of time (it's only the poorest of the poor who can't afford a carpet under their feet), the woman leaves the house, having first painted herself and her fingernails. How wonderfully vast Nature is. All the poor see of it is the speed limit signs, which they disregard before being recycled in our fodder along with their unruly cars. This woman's vagina has been pumped full of her husband's fermenting product. Her thighs under the panty-hose are sticky with the Direktor's daily slime. He likes to show that he could duplicate himself if he wanted, even if there's not much ink in his machine any more. He'd have no problem at all toasting some other, much younger crumpet under the flame of his desire. In the mountains the temperature drops rapidly. Call it a relationship, if you like, when the forest is reflected in the waters of the reservoir and the grass grows high at the window in order to soothe memories of domestic slaughter. How angry the poor can be if you pinch them or squeeze them or put the screws on (good and tight, the way the tax laws tell you). The Direktor of the paper mill never ceases to be amazed that the hordes of people who work for him all buy the same things in the same supermarket, even if they're different sizes and weights. The small village stores have long since shut down, so that the locals don't get too jolly with their sausages and beer. The factory choir (the sweet sound our industry makes abroad!) and its choral clamour of yesterday afford this man a way of rousing us to defence, breast-high, swell that chest. A kick's all that's needed to stop lust, mankind's white member, from absolutely having to spout forth. The woman is silent. In the rooms from which she is chased out solely for her sex, that unique titbit, there's howling unto heaven in memory of the battle, it can be heard right down to the fence. Man and woman have been at each other for a long time. Soon they will have to get up again and wash each other off.

Yet again, there are some who haven't shown up in the churches, where the statues drip; while others have not even been chosen. The woodman under his weather forecast and foreskin unfolds in the brief life of his wife, who works in a department store. Her career took her from school to the hay, and suddenly there were three of them, a happy family in the kitchen, the workshop of life, where they can be filed and planed into shape, there's nowhere else after all. Nature knocks humanity into a natural shape and size and takes him out to the pub so that he can burst his banks again. Back home he stands stupefied and beholds the products of his senses — the children — and wonders if he might chase them and

smash them against the walls. At times children hereabouts come to a sticky end faster than it took their
worthy progenitors to make a sticky start to their lives.
To think they're the key to continuity! While all the time
the high and mighty are poisoning the very trees, and in
fifty years' time the paper their workers make will have
been no more than a puff of smoke in the sky. As vain as
anger. As vain as a woman's choice whether to wear a
skirt or trousers; she'd just best not try wearing the
trousers at home. Like the injuries their work inflicts on
them, till one day they are no longer of any use, so too
their pleasures are fleeting. At the fountain side they dip
a hand in the jet of water. And the feeling breasts of
women sag to meet shapeless bellies in which there are
growths which the doctor tackles angrily. People don't
go to hospital for nothing. Till one day the furious are
hungry and blow out their brains with hunting rifles
that have sprouted in secret corners of their homes like
mould. At least they have found an honest master in
your good self; and you will be able to teach the child car
mechanics till it's old enough to try serious damage itself.

Frau Direktor puts a brave face on things, she paints her
face and adds a sur-face to the surface Nature's provided
her with. Beneath her make-up (where she is still
human) she crosses vaster spaces than can ever be
contained by mountains. That is why she does not rely
on mere Nature where her face is concerned; that great
force leaves her short of breath, and she has to get into
her car. Already she can see her new beau in the
fatherland of her mind, where she can see herself too,
with altogether different eyes. May her ideas not miss
the mark! From all sides she is watched by the bird-heads
of the lost, impaled on fence-posts: village women gaping
as if they had never seen anywhere but their own petty
kingdoms, where their lordsandmasters breathe the
breath of life into them come evening. They learnt from
their mothers always to look after the pence, and to stare

in awe at the face revealed thereon. What a difference between a hundred and a thousand note! A whole world of difference, enough to bridge the abyss between. The woman takes the highway's serpentine bends in her car. She wants to hear that young man say yes today, having heard him yesterday. As soon as possible. She will appear amongst us, at the foot of the inaccessible stairs. Rifts yawn wide in the mountains, but we remain below, too clumsy to handle the wildness in us. The young man will stare a wide open unlocked stare when he sees the new hairdo. It is much the same for people in these parts, caught between the creatures they care for (hundreds of dead trout in the stream because the sluices were opened too suddenly) and the work they do but don't care for. Their work is the careless gift of a factory manager. That is how we describe the progeny of the mind.

They romp and ruckus on the slopes. The lifts haul their watertight load, sealed in a plastic container, with Nature's invitation dangling, up across the frozen-stiff landscape boarded up with skis. The land seems terrible under the skis, whereas at one time it was manifold or simply folded. Snow machines retch out in front of raucous day trippers from Vienna. Every one of them thinks he's an ace on skis. Perhaps we'll stay here a while longer. Already we've been on this earth for aeons, to change it, and now it is coming to an end beneath us. Skiers only toy with the landscape, don't worry, they're not too wary: they wander upon the face of the earth, with their enormous private parts, and stamp out every fire. City folk go up to the top for sheer love of speed, and sheer speed sends them down to the bottom again. Oh, if only they could get out of themselves again! They would fly about under the sun, honest masters, showing what they have made of themselves and of others. They have commingled with others and brought forth further sporty types. Their children will take skiing lessons with their parents' piggy sutures still before their eyes. Sport, that painful nothingness — why should you of all people go without it, if you don't have much else to lose? There's no furniture here, but the jump-suits, goodies and splendour plus the absurd and ill-matched headgear will bear all before them, and, if not, just jump over the wee mountain! Behind it there's sure to be another one that will swallow up everything that fits into us. The Alps have long since started feeling the ravages of modishness, murder and *mores*: in the evenings we all roll about laughing at some clown with a concertina going through his capers for us. All about, the villagers are asleep. For them the mountains do not part when they drive to work in the morning. On their bikes, or belted tight in their tiny cars, they jolt over every bump till at last they open the gate to the employees' enclosure. Some of them make it to the top, true, if they have well-steeled footwear and nerves. Quiet, please. When all's said and done, people are at work here with their animals, each in a separate cage.

And not one stretches out a hand for one of these skiing creatures making craters in the ground to stop them. Not one is exempt from the laws of the earth, which decree that heavy things must go down, they can test it for themselves. Some of them are wearing sunglasses. They look at each other. They think of gobbling each other up. Sex is planned for the evening à la nouvelle cuisine: not much, but choice. Redly the weather steams in its basin, our forks clink, the golden heads bow down, the mountains are motionless. Thousands of offensive persons come flinging down the slopes. And a few hundred superfluous persons are busy making paper, a commodity that is devalued even faster than people are worn out by sport. Still want to read on? And breed on? No? See.

The woman ventures into town, where her husband used to park his car and inhale hot water at the sauna.

Never mind. She hangs upon his balls and cliffs, aslant his genital stairway, his very own wife, beside whom he is found by Sleep when Sleep goes looking for him. This woman is now his luxury, he pours into her till she overfloweth. The man is there to have a small matter about his person put right, and the women, in order to renovate him, have dressed in the most risqué of ways! Red lights burn at the windows of the establishment, but it is no longer as much frequented as it used to be. To snatch a breathing space, the men tend more frequently to catch the figgy snatches of their wives in their fists and squeeze them out. First they tie their pets' feet so that they'll find them again under a new dress. Now they're on intimate terms with their wives, without considering them their equals. The sun shines on the path. The trees stand there. They too are done for now.

The disease, gentlemen, is paving your way to the familiar sex, from which you always used to want to flee. Now trusting your partner is a matter of life or death. The only alternative is a visit to the specialist. To think that back then every route seemed open, and you, dear traveller, would take any one of them, happy in your immortality, and play all the tunes on your mouth organ. To think how glum you tended to be if your instrument was blunt! Now, watching, we twirl each other round on the spine and, steaming with greed, serve ourselves up in our own juice. That terrible regular visitant of sex eats at home now. He likes home cooking best. At last the man and the thing that dangles and dongs before him are one. In the old days he used to keep his wife well clipped as if she were a hedge, now he's the one who's overgrown. A bagatelle. Sooner or later, every man has to learn the knack of ramming his female partner's asshole in peace and tranquillity, for there is no other partner, this woman is quite enough. The men have plumped out now, refleshing and refreshing their senses, which are close to hand. In the old days, every woman used to be

served up as the man wished. Now he empties himself
into his own, no problem, she'll wash up after him. The
terrible visitant revels in her bed-warm cheeks. He
himself is concentrating on keeping up the erection out
at the end of his pelvis, where it bubbles and froths. He's
forever afraid of being off form and finding some
amiable stranger taking his place. Ah, lust! How one
would like to make it the cornerstone of self! But I
wouldn't go ahead and build on it if I were you.

Like beasts of prey they slink along their blossoming
lanes, casting down ramblers and rocks. With their
mighty packs of genitals these men are out searching for
a bosom where they can lay their heads for good. The
herd is still docile as yet. Their meat's still sealed in
cellophane, clearly visible, but soon, when the sun
touches and turns it, it'll bloat and grow and juice will
come from the tiny slit. And then the sun will be beating
down, the moist deposit will burst, the acrid smell of sex
will whiff across the parking lots, and eyes will be yoked
together two by two till the cart lands in the ditch and
wishes go wandering off without their master, looking
for another animal to pull along. Men shall not have lived
in vain. If they wish it, women will piss in their faces.
They lie still under the tree of sex, the planting of which
they superintended themselves, and now they in turn
are watered by the tree. If it'll get her a new brooch,
Gerti will do that at home too, if a fist is thumped into
her manured bed till her earth opens up and she relaxes
her sphincter. Pleasures such as this are available to each
and every one of us. We don't need to hide away in our
closets of wretchedness, hemmed in by furniture and
nothing but. People looking higher and higher so that
they won't have to lower their standard of living.

Time wears away lust, the desire to penetrate each other
and emit penetrating cries. What counts is to deposit a
still ampler body alongside our own dump one of these

mornings. But the weary ones, they gobble each other up, down to the fingernails. They have a better time of it, not having to be slim or to bleach their hair, they're pale enough from the machine to which they must return and which they must keep clean. And if they look about them they see waste fluid from the water supply building site polluting the stream. And everything they've done, all they have created, has to be shut down and dried out and held to their breast. And all the Direktor of this state-padded and foreign-exploited plant wants is to squirt off into his personal plague, his wife. In the interval from evening to morning she becomes a threat to him. How can he enter by the rear when he's been shown the door? Will Hubert the huntsman (or Hermann the cuntsman) ever be able to fall asleep in the acrid fox-hole where he's been caught at it? Who, if not he, would kneel before his wife, senses pricked, laying aside her folds one by one? Above, she puts a good face on things, while below he buries a bad face in things, hissing promises with his forked tongue. There is air all around the field, and women are about us constantly. We eat of them, we eat with them. No fear that this trafficking intercourse might disturb the neighbour: he's busy regulating his own stop-go flow.

The Direktor keeps a tight hold of his car and pisses. The headlamps beam upon his person. He can pump his meat extract into the woman just as often as she bends down from her lofty peak. This couple can park anywhere in his spacious house to take their lawful pleasure of each other. The woman is off to have her hair done. Beyond the mountains the sky is brightening, the pastures are being clad in day, which shows everything up better. Only this woman is lying her way into cracks in the wall, which time has forced there for her. We are one and all of us vain, ladies. Let your dresses blow in the wind and your teeth in your mouth, and fall upon your partner as if he had done you no harm for hours! Mind your language!

It is a never-ending dream for the couples. They go to work and raise their eyes from the path they know in order to look at another person they know too. And there they stand, next to each other, and one of them just has to buy that reduced tracksuit, to devalue it entirely. The path fades and withers below their feet. Their wives are all gaping wounds where they have been touched, but nowadays none of them will take sick leave lightly. Otherwise the company where we have a place of work for life and a partner for love will frown. How does the picture get there once we've punched the button? No idea, but you'd best switch off if there's a storm and retrieve your own image from the terrible slot where no one would insert even a single schilling to look at it. And yet you are alive. And oftener than you really deserve you live off the affection of a woman who has to gum and glue you together. Purely because she's hoping for a little love.

Gathered beneath the clouds, they go in at the gateway and disappear. Just made it; and in the factory they'll meet the maker. Now go home to your wife and rest, while the rubber smokes at the breakers' yards and soldering irons sweat. The metal groans, and steel entrails spill out of the cars that once enjoyed greater love than the wives whose jobs on the side paid for them. Just one more thing: don't be guided by your own taste, because you need only blink and there'll be a new model on the market, waiting for you, nobody but you! Just imagine! You'd already own one, having inveigled it with words and savings accounts long since. And that'd be it. Nothing doing. Off home with you. Got it?

12

COMPLETELY REMODELLED FOR HER suitor, the woman, topped by her hairdo, reaches the shore of the small town. She presses only her handbag tightly to her. She has left her fateful son in school. Policemen, promptly blushing at the sight of her, have very nearly been escorting her across the street. She totters. But she does not sink: an expert swimmer, beneath whom all evil is borne away on the current. In her claws, the mink coat, the woman paddles about in the work of the other paper tigers above whom two-thousand-metre peaks tower menacingly. They are the people who have torn cellulose and paper from the grip of this tough, toothless land-scape. The woman's clothes: a sempstress ought to be able to run up a simple copy of them any time. Heavens, the things she's wearing! Hacked small, the wood is stacked up around the factories and sawmills. Why is the Frau Direktor wearing stiletto heels at a time when frozen water is everywhere keeping a firm grip on the ground and on us too? We don't dare walk if the traffic light doesn't want us to. What nonsensical clothes the woman is wearing! She gets behind the wheel and tosses back a nip. She sprays something anti-herself on her teeth. Her loaned lover won't fall in the snow, he's so accomplished, a real work of art. Youth is its own reward, even if one breaks a leg. Youth laughs at its own stamina as it lunges cheekily out, clad in a fashionable coat resistant as yet to the assault of the years. Let us grant them a jolly day out on the waves of sport, rich and poor alike: all of them frequently have to drive a long way to enjoy it. To enjoy the virgin snow and a bit of excitement. The rich, mind you, want to get closer to the source of the elements (and plonk arse-down in the purity of the virgin product). It powders away, dazzling. It is as if they were earthborn. But the others strain at their leads at the factory and at their loved ones back home, and they too rejoice in the snow.

The Frau Direktor gets behind the wheel, having outdone herself. The mouths of the town mould into smiles at the windows of cafés on seeing her. She's merry. See, she pulled a bottle out of her fur! Her mouth smiles in the cold. The great and small behind the panes bow as if they thought to plunge into her heart. Young women with children and dresses hanging upon them just have to choose this moment to go shopping. They want to see something. They want to be something. Like this woman. They'd know what to do with it, that's for sure! A debacle in broad daylight at the hairdresser's, like our skiers at the Olympics: to tear the gadgets out of our hair, the gadgets we women are wrapped up with. They've never dared. To gaze without fear at one's own image. Hair, at any rate, really can be changed without any difficulty, if we don't like ourselves any more, ladies.

And we're a new human being, mild and gentle, touched by our own beauty. Fine: we'll simply carry on in different packaging. Every woman, as she grows older, will pay her price for washing cutting bedding down and having a wild time. So that it looks as if we have more hair than we really do have in our accounts. All the deeds, all the gateaux we took such pains over: when the work was done we went off aimlessly into the dusk with our forks that were useless now, we ate, washed up, and sank down upon a loved breast, one who shoved us off on four little wheels into the pantry to scrape the remains of life off the pans. And if it hasn't yet happened, we shall soon be exchanged. Just as soon as someone has shaken a regretful head, and rage has spread across the faces of the quarrellers. Then we shall have to be quiet as mice in the emptied room, as if we ourselves were already empty. We never forgive. But neither do we forgive ourselves if we want to plunge into someone else's rattling senses. It's all senseless. Someone younger will soon replace us entirely, someone bred on new-style health foods. And why me? Why, at over 40, I am hard to get. And weigh in heavier than a child, the scales groaning and straining? Me, who have always tried to address each unanticipated joy as it arrived and have bought myself a new dress.

The Frau Direktor kickstarts her car and drives cumbersomely off to catch up Michael, who can be heard on the piste by now. Laughing and yelling like a policeman, he whizzes past his friends, or crashes into them, a jolly jape. Even at night, his memory keeps all the places he goes to logged away. That and only that is what's meant when people say they're meeting others on the same wave-length, the permanent wave a terribly fashionable hairdresser has created. But watch out: don't miss the next wave of fashion. Often we may shake our heads first, but then it does go with us for a while after all. Look at my head, and don't be afraid to give something new a try. Free trial offer. We carry ourselves round in a printed bag from a sports shop. We don't have to mind how we go; the road we go on would be better advised to mind us, since we could easily ruin the vegetation for the next five hundred years. This Michael would not crack the earth open if he were to fall, as we less skilful ones would. We are not flowers, but still we want to shove our heads through the wall of Nature! Michael, though, will only be splitting his companions' sides: the whole time he's been telling them, laughing, about the funny thing that happened with this woman he reeled in yesterday and threw back again. The burden of failure lies like a load of firewood upon other shoulders, many of them, so that we can lie warm abed. We only need to set it alight. And in love a mouth encounters breath where something has just been boiled. The woman is no longer completely bright and bushy-tailed. She drags her fingers through her hair, ruining the work of other

people under whose drying hoods she trembled. Right
now, a bunch of children may be waiting outside her
house, members of a music group sent out under threat,
but so what, it's only a hobby anyway. The sons and
daughters of those who groan beneath their poverty.
Those who even have to spit in their hands if they're to
summon the energy to be fired. Already the woman has
forgotten them. And herself. And drives to the foot of
the piste, where the right of the speedier is demons-
trated. Where tourists, put down and put up with,
unshackle their gear, or, two by two like patient animals,
heave their heavy rear ends marked by the ne'er-to-be-
mended tumbles of Life into the chairlift once again.

Forwards, ever forwards. We don't want to look back,
after all we haven't got eyes in the back of our head. The
woman's high and mighty heels dig a hole in the ground.
Astounded, the winter holidaymakers float like boats
across this poster landscape where everything is in tune
and only one person is disinclined to join in the chorus.
The torrent of people pours incessantly down the slope.
Let us be more appetizing! More digestible! Lord, these
tourists. Eternally cemented into their uniforms, straying
every summer from the mountain to the beach, and, the
moment they're beached, finding it's winter again and
wanting to be up on top, where they hope to find their
bliss: being there is all that counts! And a loftier, more
conspicuous, more pleasurable overflow into the valley
below. Though they'd rather be invisible when the boss
flares up in front of them and roars like a propane stove.
Isn't it lovely, that light blue jump suit with the fur-lined
hood and a pullover red as a clipped ear peeping out! We
might be tempted to forget that nothing we're wearing
matches, nothing about our persons goes together, the
upper and lower parts, heads and feet: it's as if every one
of us were made of parts of different people. (Let's face it,
that's how we maturer women are built, somewhere
along the line we lose our shape, and then no one will

love our shape any more.) And all those different people are different in terrible ways known only to the martyred lower classes. So here we all are, martyred on our crosses but wearing our best clothes. Doesn't it look priceless!

They stand around in groups, smirking and smoking and drinking themselves empty, the disciples of sport. They have little of each other to declare as they bob at anchor at the valley terminal, smiling. The peak of their experience is: eating to live! They talk about it. Their ignition sparks light up the land more brightly than those who have to build on it. Ah yes, the tourist trade is very profitable! Now they are collecting their belongings, while the branches sag heavily under the weight of snow and daring light, barely sensed on their nylon apparel, clears a way through the beautiful snow, which lies placidly on what was once a meadow drinking water. Soon the water will no longer be able to seep down into the ground. We'll have boarded up the earth and lacquered it with tracks. Every one of them has private suspicions that he or she's the best skier on the slopes. So all of that has ended well too. In winter, when the land is supposed to be asleep, it is woken up good and proper. Noise pours from faces. In seconds people cross distances that have been measured out and reach out for parts where there is no ceiling above them and no ground beneath them. Blameless children fall by the wayside. Let's not be packed away again in our original box, let's not splay our legs unnecessarily if we've learnt how to do a perfect parallel swerve now. We can ski world champions into the ground. And that goes for our cars too, in their classes. What a day. The young people bare their heads. Snow falls on them, but they need not be afraid, it won't stick. The Austrian Winter Sports Association does not tremble before our souls: it takes a tight hold on our limbs, wounded in their pride, and pulls us down head over heels. It bandages our thighs, and next year we'll be coming again. And getting on. Let's

hope that next year lack of snow won't leave us being
shoo'd about like insects!

Like sand in the clockwork of the world we drift into the
valley. Our skis, our sharp edges which others are
forever trying to smooth off, bite hard into the firn, the
snow marked with signs: every man for himself on this
white festive garb on which we are tumbled like refuse.
Most of it belongs to the Austrian forestry commission.
The rest, a nectar of hectares, many thousands of
hectares, belongs to nobility and others who have taken
possession of houses, people who own sawmills and have
contracts with the paper mill, long-term contracts signed
in blood. Chairs on which things that have been said
acquire meaning! Wonderful. We all want change, it is all
to the good, and skiing fashions in particular change
every year, and get better and better. In haste the earth
receives the sportswomen and sportsmen; there is no
father to take them in his arms when they are tired, but
there is the Frau Direktor from the paper mill. Come
over here a little, if you can move fast enough with those
things on your feet. The light will soon be coming from
her mouth!

Michael laughs, and the sun clings onto him. In the
course of decades, the landscape has undergone change
so that it will only receive those it finds congenial. The
farmers no longer qualify and are sitting watching TV at
home. For a long time they were the surly saviours of the
land, giving rude replies to the agricultural co-ops, but
now those days are over. Change is the garb we wear
now. Our neighbours are shaken to the very limit of
their understanding. In our colourful clothing we have
become something to enjoy when we lie about on our
skis in the woods with broken limbs, skis that were once
there for wild animals to gnaw at and now merely signify
gnawing pain. But we want to be wild ourselves, too! To
shout out loud so that people far off hear us and are

startled: avalanches that contain us when we feel like
spilling over. Getting out of ourselves. Sitting in the lap
of mountain crags! And the mountain hurls rockslides at
the incautious. Nowadays the land lives off such people
and takes pleasure in the fact, and even the pubs
positively reek of our taste.

The woman thinks — and in this she is as mightily astray
as we are in the scraggy woods — that she cast a glorious
net over the young man the day before. She clapped her
frightful image upon him, and now he keeps the picture
in a breast pocket, a dart of cloth, and is forever taking it
out to look at it. Now it's time he came out from
wherever he's hiding from her. Quietly thinking of him
isn't enough for her. There's an incessant dull thud of
lust in her. And the slope promptly returns an echo of
the yodel, having no use for it. It has its own sound
equipment. On all quarters, people are squealing like
stuck pigs, as if their sharp, narrow blades are cutting
right into the very storm. No longer kept alone by the
night, when you can see nothing, the woman wants to be
dazzling bright in Michael's eyes. To make an appearance
here in one's genuine shape takes extreme courage, you
have to be strapped and buckled into your gear by the
sharp looks and skis of those on the slopes. The heels on
the woman's impractical shoes drill into the snow.
Heavens, isn't she aware of how, buoyed by feeling, she's
practically clambering and crawling up this hill? Unski'd,
I mean unskill'd, as she is, I can't help wondering which
way and how far her efforts in her unsuitable footwear
will take her. She's wet through already. The heels of her
shoes are tearing holes that it will be hard to close up. We
ladies have to sow ourselves ruthlessly on the fields, on
the parquet dance floors, where we have to prove
ourselves among the vultures. But we want a little
more of a return than just laughter, even in sport!
Wherever you go, we first have to be valid for the
journey (slot your ticket in the machine, that's right),

and for every occasion we have to be got up in app-
ropriate style so that, once open, we can be slammed shut
again. Creative endeavour is ever at a rapid end, and
inevitably we discover what discover we must: to wit,
whether we fit the furrow we've been strewn in.

This woman, enamoured of herself, inebriated, tumbles
into pits in the snow of her own digging, and there is no
hand to drag her out by her new-waved locks. Dear lady,
we are sorrowing for our departed friends, who have had
to leave for home already! But we are still there, and the
season tickets that will take us over the hills and
mountains are at our warm breasts. We don't wish to
give offence, but you've set up your safe home in the
unsafest of places, so that you might just as well have
none at all. The sun screws these youngsters by setting
too early, but in the dark they will pair off promptly once
again, too. It is our right to scale the mountains, and no
rules govern our conduct there but the law of gravity. In
amazement we swerve and give way to each other, but at
times we take the wrong direction: never gob or slash
that way or you'll get your own self straight back.

And what of the others? Just you take the average
employee out of his locker! On the ski slopes he comes
into his own, the lackey, the creature of obedience, a
being insensate yet still with a vote, who imagines he has
the right to look right through this woman, laughing.
With nothing but the voice of youth he can make fun of
her any time he likes. In the office, the young gentlemen
have to behave and beware of the boss, but here all their
pining is at an end as they fly past the pines, past Nature,
as if they were so generous that they'd give themselves
away! Immortality! Gold medals will set you free. And
anyone who takes a tumble in the slalom as he might take
a tumble in the tempests of Life will soon find that no one
will shed a single tear for him!

*

Beneath the ice on the stream there are whole clusters of trout, but in winter they're difficult to make out. Michael's friends are sitting about together, welcoming each other and looking up over their sunglasses. Michael swings down the piste in a spray. Everything's going to be fine, because some very good-looking girls have turned up now, they'll turn in and turn over and then return. They stand there indifferent to us, we who do not blossom like the untouchable snow over there against the rock face. They are still too close to the origins from which they came. All of us take pleasure in new things, but only they look good in them. They are as they are. Remote from the pastures where we fat cattle graze, ashamed of our own thighs. We have lost sight of our own beginnings, they are mantled in a mysterious radiance, hidden far beyond memory, not to be repeated. It's not just in our social positions that we're stuck fast.

But let's return to our human analysis, anatomy, anomaly: the woman rushes from her Christian Social environment and flings herself upon the student. At this precise moment his ski poles are still dangling from his wrists like an afterbirth. See: what was richly rewarded last night with an ejaculation now supposes it can venture into the light of day, looking almost human. We're not used to having the wind blow about us like this, we live in a two-and-a-half room apartment! By these toilsome tracks we'll never make it to the top where the streams come tumbling down and the skiing is top quality. You and I, we'll be seeing each other again at the snack bar, queueing among the multitudes. No home for us at dusk. A time when many are to be avoided but few to be sought out. So that, as rivals, we can lay ourselves like burdens upon each other's shoulders, heavy as weather.

Clumsily the Direktor's wife in her cloak of mink and alcohol casts herself upon her current lordandmaster's

breast. She wants to quit this world with him, spit out
the pips and start up her own Sunday supplement. She
wants to start anew, with Michael breezing lightly about
her. But let's see things as they are: this Michael can't
take this woman as she is because the problem is the way
she is, her years, how she looks. Particularly here, in the
bright light, with the tackle of all these sporting folk
grinding and creaking in the cold. But the light of love —
which goes by our side from the very start, though even
our cigarette lighters burn brighter — has fallen upon
her. And has cast her on the ground like a sack of garbage
that's burst open as it falls. And the locals laugh. Far
away the trucks go thundering by. Can you hear them?
Mind you step aside a little!

These people barely feel the need of rules. After all, their
feelings regulate their lives. The woman doesn't improve
from constant use, but if she herself wants to avail
herself of a young man, make herself available to a fellow
who lives nearby: no, it won't do! The sons of Fate
skilfully cover themselves with their hands. The woman
blushes scarlet, her face glows, she isn't there. She just
doesn't show in this young man's viewfinder. In the eyes
of this beholder she isn't beautiful. Youth, like the day,
grows and disports itself and does it with each other and
then, buckled to its skis, falls into and upon the village
enclosure. No matter what, all things present are fine by
Youth. Youth is its own performance. Everything
belongs to it. And nothing belongs to us, not even the
place where we sit in motorway restaurants and the
waiter, not deigning to attend to us, carefully fails to
register our presence. Gerti clings to Michael but slides
off his harassed plastic clothing. As anyone of his age
would have been, he was carried away a little by the
woman. He's easy-going. He likes it here. People like him
are given away in recognition of loyal custom by the local
tourist office, who put him in their brochures. Whichever
pub he may be in, the air-conditioning breathes silently

above him. But we, us extras, we are so difficult to move, we hang leaden upon our catheters, through which our warm waste waters trickle wretchedly away. Even the roads are unfriendly. We mountain hikers, naturally nurtured on the bottle and bottled into Nature's nurture, wolfing down the ham and cheese. Yes, Nature wants a little fun as well when the day comes for us to poison ourselves. Otherwise one dies all the sooner on her steep roads, of her cold products.

Michael has already moved a little way off, quickly. The light shines upon the quick and the dead, but it seems to be particularly fond of him. Our godlike Olympic skiers have already bagged two gold medals which hang about their necks while we contemplate the obverse sides: the glitter of fame like a chandelier hanging from the TV ceiling but never reaching us. Superficial though Michael is, untouched and untouching, he's still having an honest good time yawping with these lads and lasses. The woman reels in the deep snow by the barrier and sits down. The sturdy cable with bales of straw attached to it serves to cordon off the woman and all the rest who do not want to be let out of their byres for some fun and games from the sporty types who live on the boards that are really their coffins, types who taunt the skiers in heroic first place with mock acclaim: *Karli Schranz! Karli Schranz, der gehört uns ganz.* The woman's body arches into the architecture of longing, to cut the distance between herself and vanished youth. Maybe we can at least go tobogganing with our friends! But no, Michael's group has already been decided. They are constantly in each other's eyes and sometimes they even like staying at home to live in the relevant periodicals and cheer each other on in the pictures. These young men, in whose sheltering embrace the woman would so much like to spend her sleeping hours, aren't playing a game; they're hoping to be washed up to the executive levels soon. Jolly as hunters they go a-wandering in the woods.

The woman gets to her feet, staggers around, and sits down again. No good expecting her to buy the fare, she's brought along a pub of her own in a little bottle. She takes a drink. Michael calls to her, laughing, and another little demi-god who has often scarred his enemies by his mere presence reaches out an arm from his goblet (a can of beer) and tugs at Gerti, laughing, to haul her out of the deep snow. He pulls at her sleeves. Soon he finds it's taking too long. So he just nudges her from the deep end into the shallows where he himself wouldn't care to be and where the kids can be left to their own devices, they'll be back an hour later, out of the sun, roasted. When it's cloudy, animals fall silent. A bad sign. The clouds always draw in when it's time for the slaughter, so that the blood can spray out. Practically without thinking, the woman, she of the freshly gilded head, stares into the light. Now she falls over again and is dragged onward. People paw under her coat. There are children who go on and on tugging at their sex till it produces something, oh joy. The woman's new-fangled hair spreads out in the snow. The mink coat flops over Gerti. Outside the simple homes in these parts, children with heavy pails take a fall. The people built their houses by the water because the land was damp and cheap. (Like our dreams of the opposite sex!) Every day they carry up the weight of the cross on the summit in their rucksacks, so that God knows why he took all this upon him.

A little apart from the woman and her group, beginners are stumbling about, you wonder why they don't just go silently under like ships, but no, they're screaming! And why? Well, they want to get ahead, but they expected something else. Like you, whoever you may be, who think public transport too shabby. They take themselves off into the unknown, taking their pimples and crampons and thermos flasks with them. But they seem to prefer all that to the malice of the world they normally inhabit. All smiles, they issue invitations, they still have the wind to do that. These youngsters usurp the world and use up its products; they dwell in them and are in turn used by them. First it's the lungs' turn. Busily they live and learn and lounge about. Without so much as a single misfortune to cover them, these fledglings sleep, and on waking they look down at themselves, hello hello, there's one, no, two parties already engaged upon them! They've not had to hunt long for suitable partners, quite the contrary, they're the ones who are sought-after via airport public address systems and in TV commercials. They perk you up. Take any sight you can think of and face facts: these people are far more worth seeing. They are like the toxin slumbering in the poppy: a single millimetre beyond the law they really begin to blossom. There's always someone waiting, smiling, who abruptly leaves if we get too close, always a car door's being slammed, and always people are driving up to petrol stations where the poetry of gaskets is understood. Their life is swollen with the time spent changing scheduled flights (just for once to hang loose and let go, as we ourselves would like to do as well!). The very idea of it. But they're right. Youth. A whole heap of Youth! Unfortunately I am no longer one of that particular crowd. And one more thing: whatever business they're about, they're always smiling, even in the shady depths of the woods when they step aside to do their business. As empty as song they rest in the air, not even arrested by branches. So they can fall straight to the ground, and shed light on that sad place where others of more laborious build have blasted the way for a road through the forest, simply so as to ramble and romp a little. They laugh. Often it seems the best thing to do. Carefree they channel the sounds from their Walkmans into themselves and become distinctly restless because they cannot escape the music running into them. Fine by me, if it's what they like! And this woman has to get attached to an asshole like Michael, of all people, who has long since lost himself from view, though not his goals in life, needless to say. Never, perhaps out of idleness, has a woman matched his wishful image. No, what he wants is a more human place to live, say a loft, where he can stand himself up on the floor at last and still his desire for classy furniture and girls. Here, of course, tangled in the spruce roots, something of an eddy swirls about Gerti, an unedifying whirl beside the beck, where blue-collar and white-collar workers and freelance trippers regroup in the snow after they've been chased and if need be have had nails driven into their thigh bones. Why else would they subsequently claim they felt new-born after a day of sport and several of hard work?

Yes, we all take great strides forward, or else we drive off home, given the chance. But to think that this woman's eye has lit upon Michael, of all people, and that she imagines she will blossom forth beneath him, and that she would like at least to go out with him a time or two! Though she would also fancy staying in with him. Her husband devotes all his attention to his business. Aforesaid husband could easily pocket Michael, his friends, and half the gross regional product complete with the roast he's lunching on today, if his pocket weren't already full. The skiers' desires will soon be satisfied, just be patient a little, and then the skiers will be off to the pub.

Cheering and howling, the bunch of young sportsmen hurl themselves upon the drunken Gerti, hooray! They too have now taken a good pull at their own reserve tank. The mountainside conceals them, hiding them from their fellow-beings' point of view. This massive spruce is in the way as well. No expense has been spared. To prove the point they show off their solo asparagus sticks which they have pulled out of their skiing clothes, not bad if you compare the pallid growths of others who sit around crapping and doing the earth no good. They laugh throatily. They twirl their ski sticks. There are so many of them that they are a factor in the sports gear trade, in the nation's economy. They are experiencing the ultimate: they want to have a good time as they pass by and time passes by. As they fly by from the top station to the bottom. Loaded, they lean on each other, their faces turned to each other, and each has got a big tail too and stands there breathing over it. If all of us were to stick together like them, bar staff and doormen at discos could never part us! They know how to hide happiness protectively from our clutches, in a crowd. This is where our wealth has got us. Thus far we appear in Nature, which comes to us from outside. But we, not born of any spirit, are sorted according to what fine specimens we are, and have to stay outside. And the ground gnaws at our undead feet, forever having to go on.

13

THEY ARE THE PERSONIFICATION of fleetfoot life. The girls too. Not for nothing are they friends. Friends who will slander each other after they've written their doctorates and are competing for the top jobs. While all about them wretched Life, feeble children with ruined teeth and vertebrate and vertebrae animals they nurture for the slaughter, blink at the downhill racers and can only dream of Olympic golds themselves. Austria, you export factor, you'd be better off exporting yourself, entire! Send the whole package to the world of sport! We read the paper, when we poor creatures can take a chance for once too. Don't moan, *do* something! This village isn't spread out before you in the meadows just so that you can step in the dung heap.

Michael laughs loudest of all. After all, he's taken on the most of all. He may take on this woman on the downhill slope of her life a second time, or there again he may not. Yelping with curiosity like a child, he hauls out his droopy rod. Just slipped out, didn't it? The girls, who look so superficial in magazines that make them into pictures, screen off the couple that blew in from the cold, they laugh and drink and tangle together into a tight knot. In the snow there's a two-litre wine bottle and a flask of cognac. No matter what they get up to, they're attached to the mountains, and will stand there together, rooted to the spot, till an avalanche hits them. Their hopes won't be dashed. Their sex is not yet in ferment. You can drink them warm, straight from the cow. No matter. Amid the squawk of their inner voices, Gerti and Michael slip into a plantation of spruces. They are a kind of island in the grove. And there we have it. Michael demonstrates that his member is not yet properly erect, and Gerti's vagina is clearly visible in the silk, as if she were hoping she could still make it somewhere in a boat with that big a hole. Lord, what a noise the people over there on the slope are making, as if they were all one single loud yell. We can't hear any of the stupid foolery of Gerti's clitoris, which she'd like to have rubbed. All this pack of pricks have probably just been unpeeled from their plastic skins by Mother Nature! The universally valid organ is displayed to Gerti, her hands are wrenched away from her face and sex. Both are filled to bursting with angry songs, I see. The lads hold her living hands together above her head. In that position, nobody could wave to her family via the TV screen. The woman stretches out to Michael. Her face gradually crumples, as those standing about her notice. And yet it speaks of love. There are songs that say love is the noblest of our celebrations and pledges. The silk dress is shoved up to the waist and the panties, which she was perfectly satisfied with, are shoved down. And now we'll tickle the darkness till it collapses upon us with a crash. Friends have been sent round to our place to help. To make sure the labia the woman has about her person are forced apart first. To rummage in the depths, stirring things up in the ant-hill. It's as busy as a station toilet at night when the winos are shooting the breeze, stashing and slashing because they're tanked up to the eyeballs again. So now these footcloths, these doormats, all four of them ours, are parted. Making Gerti howl. So they generously fold her shut again like a brochure. Negligently. But let's just poke a finger in and then snuffle at it before the wayfarer disappears down the drain. We didn't realize how far the shadows extend into this living creature.

Through this tubular entry here, to be exact, which yet awaits proper discovery, yes, right here behind the door of shame, the hairs of which are being tugged and tucked and plucked. Pop music grants the listeners' requests, Gerti's legs are straddled as wide as possible and the Walkman is held to her ear. Now she has to lie just like

that. Her cunt is plucked at regardless, it's juicy, her
husband normally goes in and out of her with rapid
strides. He comes from afar off, we can hear him clearly.
It's unbelievable how you can stretch and flex the labia to
change their shape, as if that were what fate intended for
them. For instance, you can pout them into a pointed
pouch. And from the higher ground the hills are bowing
down from Gerti's dress. That hurts, doesn't that occur
to anyone? Right, and now laugh a bit, and pinch, and
thump, that's it. These kids get about in the world, they
like doing so and they talk about what they do. Any
permanence in the hairdresser's beautifying treatment is
already no longer apparent. Behind these mountains,
Gerti has collapsed, a butt of ridicule like her entire sex,
who switch on the electrical domestic appliances but
have no say where their own bodies are concerned. Just
as grass subsides humbly beneath the cutting blade. This
flesh parts as in a game, and then it rests, and in sleep is
rewarded still more: this is truest of the young girls,
when they laugh their own teeth tear their faces open.
Their hair doesn't need special preparation yet, it can be
enjoyed the way it comes. They are in love with someone
or other. Just as the eagle hatches its young far far up,
practically in nothingness — having first had to shlepp
the eggs the whole way up. And those who are older
detest kids. And a pair of trousers is eased down a little
way.

Well now, let's not go so far, slaves ourselves, as
forcefully to take what is ours from Gerti. Seeing that
the wind and this whole loving band have immoderately
made an immodestly blown up cloak of her. They totter
about aimlessly, there's not much to it. Now I don't know
if Michael really does have to show that his mother and
particularly his father endowed him handsomely as far
as his member goes. He struts his stuff, but it doesn't
quite rise to the occasion, his freshly-squeezed sex with
ice cubes floating in it. He brandishes it in front of the

woman. Did you hear thunder just now? So why not get out of the way and let me have a look at the video people wrathfully plumping up their genitals? Over there on the substitute bench is where you belong, where no one can see your scrawny arse and sagging bitch dugs as you labour away, blowing on the glow. Rub in the creams to rub out the distinctions between yourself and decent Grade A human beings. Go and pour forth your woes to the Gentleman one storey higher, but don't wake the dead! Apart from a swift jet, nothing comes from Michael's sting, people are drawn to him from over the fields. The mountains overhang the lake, the hands row alone. These girls stand and watch, the voice ceases to pour from their cracks, they claw at their own curls, their own wily sex that can tempt, they are ready and willing to wrap any man in it who might chance by and whom they have learnt to assess by his haircut, his clothing and his vehicle.

Michael's whole small-page ad is plugging loud specialist products. On TV the senses smoulder in little heaps. They are intended for consumption by our youngsters who sport in the snow or in the water and barely need to take a breath. Yes, this young man really is a fine rascal. Poor Gerti. Tested so wrathfully in the school of life. Mutely they look at each other. Consider each other food. The mountains are motionless, so why take the car to shove them apart? To be merry takes little. Isn't it enough for you to go playing by the river banks and the saving banks and buy yourself a place in the gilt-edged network of the sports trade?

One more word about these girls. They have just arrived (I almost said: just come) within themselves: luscious bushes of pubic hair grow like lush rhododendrons on their gentle slopes, a breeze of health comes off them, they who dwell so pleasantly in themselves and are watched through the windows of magazines. Now they lean over the woman. Heavens, they're drunk already too! At the drop of a hat they'll be off. Where were they sent from? And what do they talk to their divine little diaries about? Where do we want to be — in the curls in their laps, perhaps? Thus the mountains, where the trees ruffle, see us. Today these people will be moving on to a birthday party, where they will look at the other little well-built guests. Like children, blown in and blow-dried, they will dangle from the belts of our envious looks, ladies — ladies, you whose charms are wearing thin, you who submit to the charms of TV soaps. We can't contain the water within us once it's boiling and wants to overflow. Let's be honest, we resent their faces of many colours, while age is fading our own to the one standard likeness, no matter what costly waters we cannily wash in. So why don't you take a rest as well, on your narrow bank! Each to his own, my little dears! But these aren't the limits of our company, purely a recommended retail price, if you please.

So as I was saying, Michael has it out in the daylight, his prick, to show that he can't or won't be stopped. First he has to tank up again. Laughing, he sits on the woman's chest and clasps her arms together over her head. He dangles his noodle into her mouth so that she can benefit from his nourishment. Gerti can follow everything very clearly, and something happens in her half-dropped panties: she passes a hissing jet of wet, yet again she's had too much to drink. Laughing, the girls pull off the wet knickers they had dragged down her legs. Now Gerti's feet are quite unbound. Everyone takes a pull at the hip-flask, but Michael's prick is still limp, to be plain about it, no good pulling there. They dunk Gerti's head, that little outhouse built crookedly on to the villa of her sensations, into the water. Her dear little cunt and dear little anus are fingered and prodded, ah, if only she could be in the arms of sleep again, soon! Where do we want to be? Where do we want to stay? Like a frog's, the

woman's legs jab and snap shut. She thrashes about
wildly. She isn't really hurt, why else would this company
that never assumes liability for anything have been
founded? Michael pokes a twig in her rather bald hill for
a while, boys do love to play about, it keeps them out of
mischief. Wait, one thing more. He pours what's left in
the flask into her pussy then clips her round her ear, but
not too hard. Ow. That burns.

It is now snowing with all the heartiness we expect of
winter. The last bottle has been thrown away. Nobody
seriously wants to take a swig at Gerti, even though she
would give herself away till the green of spring shows
through. Her cunt is merely opened up and then,
laughing, we've seen this brochure before, folded shut
again. The flaps smack in practised hands. None of this is
that important anyway. Further away, up there where
we shlepped Gerti away, the skiers are still cheering in
their little lakes of beer and brandy. They beam and bawl.
The floor of the forest is already heavily soaked in their
pleasure. Gerti's skirt, in which she waits to be warmed
up amid the trademarks, has been pulled up over her
head like a sack. The suspender belts have no bad side
effects if a man fancies giving his tool a thorough go.
Michael wags his tail around in her face. She does not see
it, and beneath her skirt she awkwardly twists her head
now to one side, now to the other, thinking of Michael's
unattainable ambrosia, his jelly congealed in a perpetual
mould, to her it's no trifle. Her face, upon which trees
gaze down in silence, is got out again and the mouth
forced open. Her cheeks are slapped lightly, you can feel
the teeth underneath keeping the face in its present
shape, with an effort. Keeping in shape is what you
should do too, dear boys and girls. Though you do so in
any case, in your skintight T-shirts! With your chicaning
hands and chic caps! Let's pretend, as we watch each
other, that we're looking at a movie. Really moving. Now
they open up Gerti's top and reveal her two breasts.

They topple out of the silk, whoops! — another moving picture! Nature, it seems, has slapped down two ill-judged meatballs from its catering supply can. Laughter. After the TV show, my dear fellow Austrians, you can go off and mix with each other. Often a finer fate lies beneath soft footfall; but wherever did I stick the wallpaper? Silly me, there it is — on me! What a fool. Gerti has to prise her mouth open and suck this thing in. Incidentally, tobogganing is good fun too, but — please — never ever where people are skiing: the last upright citizens in this world, they cannot stand it if someone squatting on one dumb lump of wood disturbs them. It affronts them. Their middle class sledges, fully paid off, are in the parking lots, and they open their doors to their owners as they return from the fire a little too late, having turned a little brown. This is the very place you'll find them. See the map attached! You just have to believe absolutely in something really smashing, and then smash someone else's teeth in. And meanwhile in Gerti a fine fire is still crackling, a whole metre of pork sausage like a fire hose in her mouth. Well now, gentlemen, heroes all: let me take a look down my sights, and see if you haven't all got a cock of your own, cocked and ready to fire!

No, there are no spare parts for the moment. The storm caused by our god, sex, sends us all to our ruin by the shortest route. Leave the man his senses, so that he can make sense of himself in peace and quiet. We women have to fix ourselves as best we're able, and then hark to the distant, echoing silence from your lifeless gadgets, oh gentlemen, still trembling slightly at the thought that the guarantee might have expired. Of us the men think last of all! A stranger Michael came, a stranger he must away, and so must his thing. Contemptuously he dribbles a droplet or so off his semi-stiffy into Gerti's face, which cannot make it to safe cover in time. The lads and lasses, faces glowing with smiling and living, withdraw to warmer places too, to stretch their stamina a little before

they enter the higher working echelons. Nothing to be
done about it. So get out of the bar and into life and don't
worry! Gerti's freebie picnic is packed away again.
Michael, who couldn't even warm to a foreplay prologue,
laughs heartily. Now all of them, a refreshing stream,
propose to see who'll be first sliding down the Alps. And
so they start a war in this bright light, just so that they,
the sons of the valley, can go cracking their very own
whiplashes good and proper. Impatiently they take their
place in line with those who will soon have departed. And
even shove to the front. Not that those who were born
poor will complain! They well know the Father's
commandments. Let there be no misunderstanding:
outside the chairlift station, where the ground is strewn
with paper cups. These dimwits who have driven to
strange territory and meet there, now they're pushed
aside and must take a stop at their own inn. In themselves. Patiently queue, with all their nice long-play
cassettes that they've been collecting a whole life long.
Their princes are singing in chorus now, and much
louder! Anyway, Youth goes by all by itself, and not at all
badly either.

I've grasped . . . it. And you . . . feel warm.

These are not the children of sorrow. They help the
woman to her feet, brush her down, the snow crunches a
laugh underfoot. She has not had to suffer too too much
for the sake of these sons. Someone thrusts her wet
knickers, a postcard souvenir, into her hand. Her coat is
even buttoned up for her. Her body's nutrient production
begins to grease her hair properly. And she has already
signed the cheque, it's just that the new clothes will have
to be altered at the boutique. She's been wanting to
re-cover her body, and yet with every day that comes she
is the more aware of the heavy bags her skin has to carry.
That wasn't the way it was meant, that stuff about the
sons and daughters, the gold eggs in the nests of high

schools. We too could be knocked right off our feeble trunk at any moment! Like leafage we would fall into the beautiful gardens of the owners, mildewed, and no matter how often the Frau Direktor does her calculations she can't come up with a decent number of incinerators. Only the children, led by the angels, sing in chorus when they enter into this house on a magic carpet and laugh at their parents. We won't hear it later. Michael feels like talking now, now that it's too late. He grabs roughly inside the front of her coat and dress, and, laughing, tugs and twists her nipples. His other hand he jams between the cheeks of her behind. And then he puts a civil tongue in her mouth. He has already retracted his shlong of his own accord, to give it an overhaul. He's always glad of an opportunity to pick up where he left off. The fellow's always out somewhere wanting to be picked up! And the whole thing has been nothing but time passing. The car doors slam, they talk of pleasures and friends that have been paid for and to which one entrusts oneself, like the fitness trainers they possess or in fact are. All in vain! The angels will never be just like human beings. Only they can experience pleasure and go within themselves. Helplessly the people retch with drink. They bring it up when it ought to be having a lie down. They puke in the snow, leaning on their cars. The women fuss, the children moan. Fine. The car drives off, but the content of these people remains behind, asleep in nature, where the true and good dwelleth and goods are lied to by their own labels. In a rage they all cry out to make a stop, for ever, and hold an attractive human being in their arms, for ever. But the rulers feed the animals only once a month, and then we exert ourselves too much. Time will bring everything to light.

Gerti is put in her car. Quiet, now! How shall I put it? She has been at the mercy of hands and tongues. She almost made off, angrily shifting her sticks and belts and apron strings. A mere safety belt will suffice to hold her back.

Others in bondage have advised her to use it. Just as the artist finds his way to art, so too the village children find their way to her, to endure their rhythmical trials at the hands of this woman. The child bows over its violin, the man over the child to punish it. The works choir sings on Sunday to express itself. Many of them sing, and yet they sing as one. This choir really exists, so that the members all tug as one man at their vocal chords while the factory crouches in wait high above them. Every now and then it's thirsty and swallows up the herd, and then the pylons far and wide can hear the humming of poor people getting in line. Like children. Many came but few were chosen to sing a solo. The Direktor has his work for a hobby, so he's okay. The youngsters pour into their vehicles, now they are off to their holiday homes, where they can stuff yet more into and out of themselves. The rooms are booked out. Blessed highway, crossing the flatland, preserving the peace and quiet for all but those who live there, whose ears bleed with the racket — till they themselves can get away for a holiday.

The woman tears across the countryside. Her mind is rioting in her head, banging at the walls of the skull it is contained in, that is to say: it goes to the limit. She is chased off by the skiers, who for their part are blown back on the wind, chirping in their nesting boxes (which can sometimes be as big as wardrobes, and still there's no more than a couple of little nuts in them!), to their cages. We contemplate the peace Nature has seeded in our hearts and promptly eat it up from the carton. The light bulbs shed their solitary glow on us. The last of the litter is cleared up. The fathers of families obey their whims and fall upon their dependants. They scrutinize the remains of the day to see if there's anything left to eat. At the edge of the sullen forest a deer appears, we'll take it, it'll fatten up nicely on our sandwich wrappers. They chew it over and over, then they relax with a nice book and a nasty programme. For the last of them, who just won't stop, there's a trek up a narrow path which they will presently come plunging down again, while down on the banks the wild creatures are already slinking about to whose keeping the landscape is consigned after 17.00 hours. Out of laziness the locals stay hidden away in their houses. The men give their attention entirely to the TV set, where they can look at the animals and country-side and learn about their own nonsensical customs. The women are unemployed. The wind breezes about the peaks and soothes the pain as much as is necessary if one's to be entertained by a series about beer brewers and farmers who grow sunflowers for the oil. Yes indeed, TV doesn't pull its punches, and the viewers punch the buttons and are knocked out by what they see.

Seriously, the day isn't going to be laying on that blue for much longer. Gerti takes a lengthy break in a pub on the way. How pleasant this effect of drifting distance is! She drinks for the love of it, others drink dutifully, separated from the lovable bunch who airily want a drink just as they wanted the air to play about them as they whizzed down the slope. A whole horde of them to crown the day, they crowd to the bar and tank up, brimful. Once again Nature is simple and monochrome. Tomorrow it will be woken by human voices once more and will merrily hammer the public down the pistes. Ah yes, the public. The public has shed the blanket of Nature but is still wearing its today of many colours, the pub currently on duty is completely stuffed with these tourists. A brawl that's seething around the drink source is quietened by the barwoman. How nice, from far away we come, tumbling from mountaintop to valley, and already we're full of beer. A couple of woodcutters, the most amiable of those who tend the mountains, are already making trouble in the bar, egged on by the city folk, and will presently, like axes, split their wives open. Gerti sits silent, forehead furrowed, amid the party, who have their own snack with salad garnish to get stuck into.

Tomorrow or even this evening, this woman will be standing outside Michael's holiday home spying in at the windows to see his friends making good use of what is his. And she, spurned, will vanish, no one knows whither, into the distance, like a fleeting thought. While her husband deforests the region and murders music. I'm cold. They've screwed one into the other, rummaging about in all the garbage for that treasured picture which they acquired only yesterday in the photo store. Only yesterday. And today they're already on the look-out for a new partner, to charm him into smiling please before they press the release. Yes, us! Torn and tormented, we become visible, and we want to look good for others, to think of what we paid for our clothes, we no longer have what we paid and we notice the lack when we have to undress and caress our partner in love. But for the time being this woman is living on alcohol; and the harvest of other people who drink too, the merry multitudes, is not for her to reap. There's a slight dispute over her mink coat, which a skier has trodden on, but it's soon settled. This breed of people beneath the farmhouse-style lamp: how they do contrive to show off their shapes within the colourful plastic limits they've set themselves so that their forms and norms won't run over and out (and certainly not the models from which they were constructed). They decorate themselves wall-to-wall like their flats and take themselves out.

There's plenty going on, it's divine. The woman takes an unaimed step back. A glass is shoved across to her, the day seems almost in a hurry, it is already dusk over the mountains. The poor popular opinion is sprayed at Gerti like water from a child's hand. Ponderously the poor people of these parts are leaving their nearest and dearest, to be spilt from dirty hands in the pubs, to gush forth like springs because of what they put inside them. But this woman had best be off home. They won't have her drinking here. She'd best be quiet. This is where the

herd live, complete with their good shepherds, see the
TV pages for the complete programme! The Frau
Direktor is a bright cloud, at least that's how she looks,
sinking from her seat to the floor, where she makes her
bed and lies in it. The barwoman kindly takes hold of her
under the armpits. A small stream puddles from Gerti's
chin and spreads. This can't go on like this day after day.
From outside, Nature gleams magnificently one last
time, and the herds of Nature's users head patiently
pubwards, glad to be able to raise the elbow at last
instead of having to rebel at the lashes of Olympic
broadcasts and be sent skedaddling across the hills. If
these people are left alone, you'll see how quickly their
true charm fades, which is that they look like film stars
and look truly charming in their own photo albums,
which is where we assess what we expect of ourselves.
But here the waves spray up against them and they have
to compete with locals all cut to a single format. They
win by means of noise, colour, perfume and money. A
song is struck up, the time of day has a-changed
abruptly, the weather too. The wind is howling through
the crystal ice hanging from the trees. Even more people
claw hold of the woman's hollows, look, now two men
are lifting her to her feet. Their loose change empties out
over the woman. A glass of wine and one of schnapps are
paid for her. They find pretexts, unable to conceal their
coarse sexual parts, to feel Gerti up all over. A flood of
laughter from their wives, who are also readying their
hairy crevices, quickly, before the light changes, and
taking up their positions. They are all still dripping with
Nature, that is how much life they have soaked up. And
it has cost quite enough, too, sitting like islands in this
bar and vomiting. One man gives a woman a piggy-back
for a bit of fun, she reddens between her thighs, which
she squeezes left and right against the man's cheeks.
Nobody wants to be missing this. They hop about, even
the best of floor shows has to be over sooner or later. Just
a short way, laid back in seconds with a little effort, the

genitals open, and already they're inside each other and squeezing the tube, whimpering for salvation, and their bowels are thunderous with what they have put away for the wilder times to come. In the dark, the first of them are already overspilling from the fetters of their clothes. Gerti's bust is pinched; as jolly and harmless as vegetables, we thrive in our lordsandmasters' gardens, ladies! On account of the higher regions where we dwell. Only to be pleasantly surprised by the instincts that shoot out of our ski pants.

Heave ho. Now the woman's sitting properly on the bench again. Another glass, in which the alcohol is rapidly growing old, is shoved across. She swipes it away with a sweeping gesture. The trouser-wearers who bought it her yell in fury and shake the woman by the arm. The barwoman sends a girl to fetch a rag. Gerti gets up and sends her purse flying on the floor, and people instantly start to rummage in it, their sweaty faces clouding at the sight of the money. The poor crowd in the back room and remember their work, which once spread its legs to them unforced. But now they no longer have any access. Oh, if only they had! Now they are at home all day long, busy with the dishes. And the others in the pub? All they crave is good weather and wicked snow. Tomorrow in the mountains they will lead dashing lives again, or else merely splashing lives if the temperatures rise steeply as the forecast said and it rains. The barwoman gently followeth the path of righteousness. With Gerti tucked under her arm, it is as if she were walking on the water, across the scummy froth of day-trippers floating on the surface. Just see with what certainty these travellers, born of the void, load themselves with gifts acquired at sports trade fairs and go off to their deaths in the mountains. A national anthem is thumped out, without any trace of embarrassment. The singers have but little in common with sirens: maybe the sound, but not the looks. But they go on and on singing, let 'em have it! Local people who cannot even work at the paper mill sit stunned before their screens and stare at the canny invention of themselves — does no one have a heart for their sorrows? And why are they divorced and dismissed from life even before they, plus their skis, can be safely stowed in the cellar?

In a state such as this one really ought not to drive, alone or even in groups, otherwise one won't be safe from oneself as long as one lives! But Gerti cuts her coat to fit the cloth of her modest privates, and pushes off from the bank. She puts her back into it and belts up. Free and easily she indulges in her feelings. Michael: now we'll go and fetch him out of his house before he goes cold. Presently this woman, impelled by her senses, will be howling outside a strange house because no one's at home. Let's move on. Switching on the lights is quickly done. In the number in which we usually remain, one, solo, single, but never mind, she drives after her quarry, the other drivers on the roads. As if by a protracted miracle, nothing happens. Wearing their homeshirts, the lordsandmasters rumble and grumble because they're kept waiting for their dinners, the dogs attack visitors and keep their jaws healthy and exercised. Which is why we all like to live in our own places and keep our own pet animals, ourselves, in safe keeping there. Just now and then we take a timid pull at someone else who claims to be brimming over with sweet sweet desire. But if ever you really do desire something of him, you don't get it!

14

THE DROPS OF GRAVEL spray up in front of the house, the dogs leap at our throats, and the door is opened. The woman even takes a few steps further, towards the balmy light that plays radiantly about her warm, waiting husband. The children have long since been sent home without the comforts of music and rhythm, and now they are half emerging from their lairs, beaten by their fathers. Relieved at seeing the springs of art dry up at the lips, and cheerful as in family photographs, the children have already attacked each other on the forest path, tearing each other's bodies and clothing to shreds. One oughtn't to get the neighbours together too often, all they do is make a nuisance of themselves! Everything the Herr Direktor wanted, he now has again, his word is our command. The kisses crash from his mouth. He holds his spoonful of distraught senses under the light, but nothing becomes heated. He kisses his wife like a mother licking her calf, his tongue even wants to get into her armpits. Automatically he warms at the sight of her, but for the time being his moist figure remains closed. He is built like a mountain, and streams have already coursed across his brow, though there's no comparison to what his workers are cursed with when, the mark of their health vacation upon them (insult and injury added to their lives), they receive the letter in the blue envelope. Not one of them, though, would see his wife as this inflated Direktor, who wants to channel her back between her banks, now sees his. What has she got there in her pocket, it's only her wet knickers, which he throws on the hall floor. As he so often has done in the past. Usually the servants do the mopping-up when the water in the tap's got out of control again. The charwoman will remove this sign of life tomorrow. Gerti has plenty of room to run around, it's time she was stabled. The boy, who's been running around to various stables all

day, now shoots out at his mother, his babble all too
horribly comprehensible, sweaty with the vexation he's
been causing his friends. Heavenly homely things about
Mother are sent across his lips, Mother for her part is
sent from heaven. She is the parcel whole peoples have
to carry and to fear. Who pushed this family's button
again? To set the realization in motion: there are three of
them, at the end of the day, when they bed down snug
against the weather. The family: the woman is no longer
sober, goodnaturedly it is put on her account by Father,
who has the chequebook about his person. His property
is what he loves dearest. Smiling, the Man strokes the
woman, but a mere second later he is grubbing about like
mad, like a terrier in a newly-discovered earth, under her
coat, pawing at the cleavage of her dress, which he wants
to have off this naughty woman right now, oh and
talking of having it off, her cheek is lovingly stroked by
his fingers, as if the creator had broken his pencil and
now life itself had to correct the job he started. The
woman can't cope with the steering of her automatic.
She is learning to walk, and listing badly.

Which of us would not gladly be forgotten on the
meadows of life, only to re-appear suddenly in the rubble
of his clothing (all of it small and standard size like
terraced houses, though we wouldn't want to change,
not even with a king)? To give oneself over entirely to
another who comes by at just the right speed to make our
passing acquaintance! To be singled out of the crowd, the
tracks that lead to money! To fall upon the child who has
made his blessed appearance at last is more than a mere
thought to the woman — yes, the heavenly hosts want to
celebrate now, a holiday amid vultures and fiddlers! Off
to Vienna, to the concert! She rollicks with her son on
the hall carpet, pretending to play, but her hand is
already grabbing roughly under the child's waistband.
The Man forces himself to smile, because he wants his
wife to himself again, that is, if he can kill off that much

life all at once. We shall see. Already his determined lump
of meat is hanging weightily, slung from his hip, heavier
than the head with which he thinks and sees. Now there
is a link once more already, but it won't stay put. The
flesh often compels one to wait things out for a long
time, as in a long-distance coach with the curtains shut,
racing through the night, its windows passing other
windows, and, since everything is in motion, people can
never meet.

The Direktor already has his hand in his trouser pocket
and is stroking his truncheon through the cloth. Very
soon his generous beam will jet upon the woman. And
the boy is beaming too. It is not simple with them, the
child is already crumbling like petfood under Mother's
cutting edge, slicing sternly into his flesh. Mother
giggles, her hair in the dust on the floor, which the
woman of the house does not concern herself with. The
child would like to tell of the rotten things his playmates
did to him. But Father hasn't got as much time to love
children as you have. Helpless, he kneels over his family,
over the one small item amid the huge entirety of his
creation. They all laugh heartily. They are tickled by
Father, first the one and then the other, as if he were out
to shake the life out of them. All of them go on laughing,
the Man is less and less touched. What does he care about
the kid! He'd rather take aim at Mother's lap, he wouldn't
mind sitting there himself. To the child, neither good
fortune nor ill matters much, there must be something
to be done about that. Time the boy learnt a little
discipline, or better still, time he went and tidied up his
room! In times of illness Mother is always the one who
does the soothing. And women even have to preserve
the Man within themselves, lay him out in the chapel of
rest, safe from the fire storm which throws bodies out
into the night like dogs, to do their business and sleep
well afterwards. Opulent Christmas decorations are
hung on spindly twigs. The main thing is to have lived, to

have been brightly inscribed in the tablets, and as for what one has eaten, from one end of the sacramental menu to the other —! No, here on this wallpaper there's nothing but Taste! Our son, our audience, is already familiar with body-wrestling and finger-painting from many an occasion in the past. He extorts a promise from Father in which sport, his god and idol, plays the principal part. Alluring promises will call upon him. He will be summoned forth by carpets of exciting snow laid out upon the remotest mountaintops. I mean, it will be exciting to see all those skiers racing across the ground to the centre of the world. The child is promised an experience, for Father is expecting a good deal of Mother's body and its ramifications stretching out into the night: this landscape cannot accommodate more than five thousand!

They strut brimful in their functional trousers, the lordsandmasters, and the son is already making his own contribution too. This child, whom Mother cannot reproach with growing too rapidly, after all, she fed him with her own frugal self. This child, a member of the fresh generation, has been brought up by his mother, *wound* up, and now he can't be stopped, he just keeps going! But now for the lordsandmasters, of whom the Direktor is the highest. His prick can be born in seconds at any time from a warm bath, be pulled out and do its work, and then be reeled in again, contented, by Fate, wherein dwells the strength to play tennis, ride a motorbike and bustle about other such business. When you walk it jiggles, gentlemen. Men try for a great deal amid the weak branches, but I am alone. The child is thinking about a period in the history of the earth which unfortunately he is unable (too late!) to experience retrospectively. A while ago, Father fetched out an encyclopaedia and bent pedagogically over his carefully calculated number of child. Anything more from a child would perhaps deflect Mother's interests too much from

Father. Father wants to tie his wife to the bed himself, venomous as disease: God is mean, but he's not the one I mean at the moment.

Like a bell the Direktor rings over his seated group. Outside the trees stand dark, waiting. The family is reconciled, heavily and discourteously the scrotums hang in their very favourite disguises, in paper-lined cupboards, in the balloons of underpants and tracksuits. You just need to reach in and see, everything can be fetched right out again. The sex we belong to, each to his own — as elastically as the rubber band that keeps the poorer bunches of people (they do not count individually) all together, it snaps out of the sack when the lonely man addresses himself to his property as to his shadow, which is the sole one of all living things that fits his measure precisely. The bundle of life, right, sags from the body and we feel fine. Those who want a lot will have to go and buy themselves something. Even the boy: already he's glowing like a real man who bows others and bows to others. He goes from the one to the other, pointing to his own person, which cannot be improved, and carries on along his own envious track, whizzing past us at high speed. The mere impression of it is a very deep one. Yes, this boy may be small, but he's specifically designed as a man, I believe.

Now he's still just a wretch, a brat, so small, but he beats on our eardrums and sends us flying to the poor neighbours, who would complain if they dared. Lovingly Mother bows her mouth to his hair. Father is already becoming inexhaustible, he can hardly contain himself. It's what he keeps concealed from his employees at other times, now he can't help squeezing his instinctive urges tight. He shoves up to his wife from behind. The woman bends contemptuously forward so that life stirs in her depths. With laughter, since his mother's tickling him, the boy shits himself, dumping his dung in Mother's face. Never mind, we go on frolicking about as if we'd just repeated, damply. The woman really has to watch out, but it's too late already and she's half exposed at the rear while at the front she's still sucking up to the child, telling him nicely to be a good boy and tidy away his toys. More this man does not dare, yet still he wins. Like a low-flying aircraft he strokes his wife's behind. Like birds flapping against the light. Today Father can sense his health roaring within him, winning free extra goes. Secretly, under the camouflage of his house jacket, he places his swollen warhead against the slit in his wife's arse, where he thoroughly examines what is at his disposal. He only needs to plough this one furrow, thus the farmer helps the good earth. None of us has to bear the burden of life alone. But why does no one help him buy a car, so that there's something to carry the load companionably with him? Let us look with our eyes open at each other's sex, so that we shall be calm and slender, just as we try so hard to be with medicines and diets. Zealously competing with the others who have come to lay their own spoor. Even at the open door, the Direktor is still pondering which entrance to take, to run himself in, what an honour, to be offered up in a sheaf! Oh God, how beautiful to be a heavy load in a cart stuck luxuriously in the mud for a good wallow. Some vandal has torn down the traffic signs!

The family go on kissing and farting. The time of blissful waiting is over and happy words are in the air. The voice of the king of the house oozes out, it becomes a battle, which he wins. He gets carried away by himself, heaven came close to forgetting the workers and employees who have been well and truly screwed by the boss on high and his holy church and have to stand in their byres, well-proportioned, well-appointed, angrily jangling their bells and chafing at their ropes. What? They don't even refrain from kicking their one sole space?

*

The woman knows where her husband's shoe pinches, the one he will kick her fence down with in a moment. Sometimes he can hardly wait till evening and tells her to come to his directorial office at the factory, where this bird of prey can contain himself no longer and angrily desires to move into his own homeliness. He reaches into the clouds of his sex and it grows, like fire. The little winner is already being pulled out of the little room above the trouser legs where he has been lurking till he is shown the voucher for a trip of a lifetime, to the golden rain in her apron. Happiness for the owner, from far away his dogs can already smell him and are at each other. Every day's a holiday. Will sleep at least find us today? We have earned it, waiting in silence on the mountaintops under our warming layers so that we do not stamp loose any planks of snow. Just think of the many folds in men's shirts alone, from which men can tip out their sacred streams!

And Gerti's stylish clothing is breached today for the umpteenth time as well. The lordsandmasters and their bellows, with the help of which they can make a loud noise; in summer the breeze is mild but in winter we have to take our own breath. The child almost fails to notice that he has come among us and is being kicked. Won't it be time for dinner soon? Will the Direktor have to let his wife out of his clutches for a while yet again? Does he want her completely sober? Mutely the animal and its rope look at each other. The Direktor can do even more: mix his wife's body, in all its shapelessness, on the kitchen table, just as it suits his dough, which will rise when covered. Thus the family makes its own food and the earth its creatures, thus the guests bid their farewells on the thresholds although they have been well fed. Gentlemen! You are strangers to me as well, it's true, but you throw yourselves about so that the nets squeak. Plates of sliced *wurst* crash down on the tables, the family sit, the weighty wedges of bread with clearly distinct grains, coarse and costly on plates rimmed with grains of gold, they have all foregathered here before so that Father's will be done. First he will spread thickly on his wife, and then, still smiling from the day — after all, he has earned his bread and now he is giving the bread to his family — then, right, the heavy drumsticks will beat down on the woman's hollow-sounding pelvis. I believe myself, but I don't believe in myself! Anyway, let's observe the holy days, and let us have the works choir sharpen our instruments! The child must live, that is how things have turned out. Abruptly and without warning, just as the sun sometimes strikes with lightning speed. High on the peaks it is already lighting up for tomorrow, but we the salaried, we who matter, we who are on the pay lists of the paper tigers, we have already had our crackling fire today, we held our bodies close to it till they almost dissolved into light and nothingness. My only advice is: make sure there's something to drink, then your worries are over!

A little ebbing sound is still entering from outside, but after all it is late, and the private sector is screening itself off to entertain itself alone. Those who have to provide the food and entertainment in the little houses above the rushing stream, where they rattle the crockery, forever half begotten, half ill-bred: yes, we women, right! On our own territory. All we can do to make more of our men is stuff them full. Now the family lock out the animals, who can no longer come shying in to us from the dark. And in the village, too, eyes are now being covered everywhere, you just keep your eyes on your own paper! Tomorrow they will all make paper out of the trees of the vicinity, as if it were a holiday. In the mean time, the Direktor is even forcing them out of the alliance he forged with them and the union. Only those who sing the right notes get the right notes in their bag. The misshapen assembly rooms in the county town pubs roar with applause when they perform there, long since

planned as a dish, amiably shuddering at the noise
they've baked themselves, as if they meant to gobble
each other up. Again and again some portion of Man is
climbing onto the woman who belongs to him, to tire
himself seriously out. Thus they hang like rocks from
their brood and from their spouse's breasts. They're
used to it. A stroking hand that sometimes comes out of
the darkness brushes them, briefly, as if it were a branch
armed with fruit. If only they could remain lying empty
just a moment longer (then they would occasionally feel
the breeze)! Let no one pick up the empty bottles right
away! Now the women are using their weapons to
flatter, so that they will be given a present, a new dress
for their inconsequentiality. They please by their capacity
for endurance, but they do not please many. And then a
burnt goulash promptly becomes an entire world.

We'll be in touch taste hearing sight and smell.

When the door has been locked, Gerti too begins to calm
down in her little fortress of curtains. But is that any
reason for the Direktor to get violent? The child races
from one to the other, puffing itself up. Father wants to
make the child a gift of oblivion, he picks him up by the
fly and drops him on the floor. He wants to throttle a
social choke from Mother's gorge at last. Quick, put in a
finger! Only the child, played by a boy, is still bothersome, gushing truths from his likewise throttled throat:
he wants a present. What cavilling criteria went into the
choosing of this child, anyway? The parents are black-
mailed and sit silently on each other in their beautiful
residence. The supply of child language seems inexhaustible, but it is not very varied, and only involves
money and goods. This child makes a plausible wish for
whole whirlwinds of technical appliances, tootle tootle
tee! His language stumbles out of all the hollows Mother
has fixed pictures of animals over. Mother loves this
child because they both obey the same law, which says

that not the earth but Father begat them. Whole catalogues of merchandise shoot out of the child. A horse could be bought as well. And the child wants to be absolutely at one with one thing, which isn't the voice of the violin, it's sport. Goods become words become money. Father has to let go of his trouser sack again, in which he is restraining his thing, one really cannot pass this woman by without doing something. He'll lick this kid into shape all right, perhaps drag him in to dinner by the hair? The TV set is a source of sound and vision, an octopus stretching out its tentacles into the room, enabling Youth to recognize itself in the image of sundry famous persons. It is very loud. The club spokesman angrily shouts out his decision: that all three were made by one and the same father, true, but were made *up* by me!

Mother lurches about in her alcohol-soft body and knocks against her household utensils. Without any necessity, this family buys its surroundings. Just look at this peace! The tables are bending beneath the glow of the table lamp, which is shining on the secret, sacred foods. What a homely country. Father's half-stiff tail is laid like a retriever, good boy, between his thighs on the edge of the armchair, the glans half peeking out, the railings bending under it. It falls from out of men, where their innards begin, where they can make more haste less speed, and on and on they chase through the undergrowth. No, this sex will not lie down to sleep till it has roused itself up and thoroughly rained itself down. That's how they'd like it. Father whets himself on his seat: how variable and how lovely is the valley between his thighs! How long it's been, and how long it *is*. The woman gazes ahead, and sometimes slaps the table. If she had her own way she'd promptly be off after her latest desires and storming into that considerable prospect called Michael. That path is now closed to her, I fear. She murmurs dark words from her scarcely open mouth. The student's holiday home, that place of pilgrimage for Gerti's flesh, we'll still have time to drive over there later. The children do not sing in the houses and do not clap their little hands, nor does the sun dare venture anything any more. Silence falls. When, I wonder, will the woman grasp the urgency of her local security organ?

The child buffoons about, now wound up into a total beast. Invariably before he has to go to bed, when one has so little interest in supper, the child starts flinging himself about, in sheer physicality. Mother too lays her head violently on the table. Her gaping wound is connected with Michael. She indicates that she will not eat anything but will have something to drink. Father, who is bursting to be off hunting, is already upping the tempo in his he-man clothing. He finds the child a nuisance, here he is in his own house, after all, where people die if they don't make it to hospital in time. The last workers escape the weather and hurry into their blessed parlours. Soon it will be completely quiet. Father's prick, that herculean muscle, feels the call of Mother. The lordly dog is still lying asleep, but soon he will have the scent in his nostrils. Upstairs the child will be talked to about school. Then the doubled-up woman will be pinched in the warm flesh of her shoulder, she will be taken by the shoulders and put upright again. Nowadays the child is increasingly acting the self-appointed boss at dinner. Disturbed in his desire, Father sinks deep within himself, indeed we see that Mother too has arrived here, only to carry on and then return. These people cannot sit still, which is generally the case with the uncannily rich from foreign parts. Nothing keeps them in one place. They drift about with the clouds and the streams. Their crowns rustle above them and their purses bustle. Elsewhere things are better, and they bare their breasts to the sun. And always the same answer to the question: who's that on the phone? The child becomes an even greater nuisance, polishing his lists of presents for his birthday, though he doesn't plane away any of his wishes. Father does things the same, on principle. He will refresh Mother with his bubbling spring. Life swirls about his ankles. Indeed, in the heat of his senses, which no rubber could contain, his body is at rest, and the fires flicker prettily from his figure. The child makes a great many demands, so that most of them will be met. His parents have finally been stowed away in the midst of their sensations by the sleeping car conductor (with the countryside flying past outside, and their urges growing too big for them and growing out into the open). For different reasons, they want the child to shut his open mouth. Agreements are violated. An hour of violin practice isn't the end of the world. Now the woman does eat a tiny little mouthful. The child won't be grown up for a long while yet. So let's get ourselves ready instead!

They can't sit around together in the altogether, the child would disturb them. The child is damned to seventh heaven. He has no secrets from his parents, spluttering the milk about behind his remaining milk teeth. It is quite a strong bond, the architecture that secures him to his parents, this child. As a matter of fact the son isn't only a nuisance when he's on the drip of his violin. He is always a nuisance. Superfluities of this kind (i.e. children) can only be created by the kind of rash actions that bring troublemakers into the house, so that they can start to shine bright and stupid as lamps from out of their awkward language. Instead of everyone being able to do it with everyone else in every conceivable hole in the place. Father wants to drag the fabric off his wife at last and run dashingly down her hill, but no, the child pervades the room like a holiday, his horn resounds throughout the entire house where all things conduce to love and particularly the specific construction of Father, who, like the big settee in the living room, is obviously suited for love. How nicely these commercial travellers of sex flower by the wayside, these protected little plants, please do not pull them up, they'll be on their way of their own accord! Hide in the woods, but don't tread on their feet, amid all that green they can be incredibly poisonous!

In the kitchen, Father tosses a couple of tablets into his son's juice, to silence this fellow who's eternally on duty, just for once. After all, his son can't do much with his juice yet, but Father, oho, once there's peace and quiet he'll thrust from his suit into Mother and tramp along the well-trod path. God sends his ramblers far and wide, up hill and down dale, till they lay each other waste for good and can continue the journey wih the children at the family fare. They sing when they make their appearance and don presumptive sheaths, when they leave the organ they leave their own dung heap behind. That is what the regulations governing the lay-bys of our life say, and in the process the countryside remains lying in the valley, unattached. Down the path that descends from the mountains, just for us, Father will come, turning in for some refreshment at Mother's dairy, where he can drink it on draught. Not even a Direktor gets a special made-to-measure job. These nipples have been well covered up by time, but they feature wonderfully in his everyday life. The child had best lie down to sleep on the house at last, when he's pretended to play the violin a little more. That's it now! We're off to bed. Just one more lullaby for Mother, who can no longer properly make out her son before her own face, though. How often photos have been taken of that face! The child laughs and yells and fights a bit, till the very last of the pills has flowed into his blood. Yes, this son babbles as if he were planning to wallow within himself in the limelight of the evening, in the sauce of his wealth. Not bigger boys nor stronger boys dare defiantly pull their things out in his presence. In their houses there are cages, right up beside, where human beings eat too.

Mother tries to avoid intercourse with Father's sex, that devastation by means of which he constructs his works in her, with the support of the holy federation. She wants to dwell, yes, but not be visited.

What wouldn't we do to escape the countless speeches from the branches of the child, get into an escape account where we too could finally lie down and, like money, increase in our sleep? It is as if this bottle had been uncorked for good. Nimbler still than the ramblers themselves are their recollections, their bank statements clearly speak of a mountain of interest and sore interest rates. The boy had better sleep and be smoked now, as far as I'm concerned he can skip his bath today. Ah, at last, didn't I say so, at last he's stopped blabbing and is reclining in the armchair. Just now he was cheekily holding forth about the things he knows, and now he is already covered with air and time as if he had never existed. Everything, for nothing is in vain, flows into a trickle of drink from his lip and down his childish chin, where his smile flowered. The child, now that he is finally quiet, is given an inarticulate hug and kiss by Mother. There'll be peace till tomorrow. The main thing is that their son has been knocked out of the way. That child has well and truly surrounded us. At a time when we're busy, with all our orifices, gumming ourselves together in our current situation, which is love. The child's room is made of rough, heavily laden walls, Father carries his son up and drops him out of his clothes and onto the bed like a soft bolster. Whatever lies, sticks. The child is already sleeping, too tired to spray any more sparks from his little tail today. The grown-ups exploit their affinity and paw at each other's gills, to show that age cannot stale them. They are not inhibited and reap the harvest gladly, they have nothing more to lose. Like insects in the sky, Father will presently go into a dive, right into the freshly-cut grass. In less than five minutes he'll have impaled his wife in his lap, which is a miracle,

clumsy as he is physically. Gentlemen, you've sprayed
your hoses around quite long enough! Now get the Ajax
and use it, on your knees, in the evenings, in the haven of
the house. Men: their eyes have been poked out and now
they're always wanting to poke someone.

This child is so young, and already gleaming (dreaming).
Tenderly Mother lays herself in the child's bed, as an
extra, is it going to be a loving night? No, she will soon be
extinguished beneath the rigid muscles of her husband,
who wants to skim his own cream. The child is already
fast asleep. Mother tires herself out with pointless kisses
which she spreads across the blanket. She kneads the
slack tallow of her son. Why has he stopped flourishing
for today? For his spirit to flee so fast is unnatural. After
all, she knows the child exactly. What tap did Father turn
off? But Father has long since withdrawn to his hobby
workshop and is pumping juice into his piston so that he
will feel on high form. He poisoned his son's juice with
sleep, so that the child might dwell in soothing night,
protected by his sports heroes and chemistry. He will
wake up again all right, to go slithering over the hills and
far away, but right now he has been taken from his
mother's side. And Mother has to stay with the child, for
there's no knowing what comes next.

Gerti squeezes under the blanket, places her kisses
beside the child on the pillow. She rummages in the
entrails of the cover, is it gradually dawning on her that
she is caught by the heel in her husband's binding, with
no hope of rescue? To get in the track now, silent, and go
down the slope! Only that binding still holds her to the
mountains, till she sinks, mournfully. Now Father is
already in his workshop, busy with the loading gear, a
good bottle is never spurned. Is that a right that Nature,
which gave it us, takes away from us once more? A while
later he is standing at the toilet, pissing it all out again.
Meanwhile the woman, cringing in her coat, is already

running out of the house. Like a farmer hunting shame-
ful rodents she races across the front garden, backtracks
without a moment's thought, and takes detours. As she
runs, she has torn the car key out of her bag. When will
the time that lies ahead finally begin? Already she is
sitting in the car, the heavy rear end of which will slither
away when she drives off, yanking the vehicle unsteadily
out on the federal highway. The motor in the dark
startles the last lost souls as they totter homewards to
answer tenderness with brutality. The headlights are
not turned on, Gerti drives as in a dream, since the sunny
places are still far away and the hills all familiar and
distant. Meanwhile the child is blossoming in his bed and
letting himself go in his dreams. The Direktor is expressing himself on the toilet. He hears the sound of the car
and runs onto the terrace, his prick, manipulated with
three fingers according to regulations, still in his hand.
Where is the woman off to? Does she want to get beyond
her thoughts in the midst of life? And you, gentlemen,
gripping your drill heads, how can you put your longing
into words? The Direktor gets into his Mercedes. The
two heavy vehicles plunge out into the countryside,
making ferocious amends. Meanwhile, those who live
along this roughly 3 km track are falling upon each other
in love, there's a slight roar from the equipment of the
unsubtle employees and already they're done yet again,
through with the gestures of love. Yes, the guests of
love! They don't feel at home with strangers. The two
cars race along one behind the other. They climb modest
slopes and slide down again. How happy we are that the
motors under the bonnets are so powerful and can sweep
aside the youngsters returning home from discos in their
dangerous horsepowers as if they were toboggans. Just
now, the Man didn't even have the opportunity to paw
the woman's tits. They drive. Today there is no growth
in Nature any more, but perhaps a new delivery of juice
will arrive tomorrow. There is snow on the ground, but

there will be fruit again some time or other on this tree, the esteemed name of which I do not know.

The Direktor has got all his natural products together and speeds after the social amenity of his wife. He MUST catch her up. Full steam ahead, they both helterskelter along the roads. Soon Michael's holiday home appears by the roadside, oh you dear people who did not cross our paths today, how lucky you were! In the brightly-lit windows an officer of style, largely proclaimed to the dark. The many worn-and-torn parts of the human body, please see for yourself, can be transformed with the help of industry and foreign concerns into a pretty impressive colony of holiday homes where we can take our many and various interests for walkies on a lead. And up front our heavy steel muzzles peek out. Where the waters of desire flood upon the meadow, the gentlemen outgrow themselves by almost twenty centimetres. Then they lead us along their narrow path, and declare they won't stop till their electricity, gas and time have run out. Once in and once out, and then they take a rest.

15

MICHAEL OFFERS A THREATENING smile from his illuminated zone where he flows about beyond the vast panoramic panes of glass. His world is well disposed, at his disposal he has sufficient driving skills, and he has tiled himself up, young and saved for at least three years, with his shiny, sanitary life investments. He will not open his door now for anything. Noisily, two people sink on his doorstep, where normally the sunshine faces of friends make a stop. It is impossible to reach Michael. The woman kicks the door and hammers at it with her fists. What was appears to have been nothing. All those things he said and did with her, all in vain! But people are never at a loss for words, nor is there any more than words concealed in them. Snow begins to fall softly. That's all we needed. Contained in his fine fibrecast of clothing the student stands at the window looking. The spell of night has already been partly broken by him. This young man owns several skiing get-ups, and generally speaking he likes getting it up, he wants to climb higher and higher, to go far. With a faint jangling, and sporting trademarks on which he even sits, he makes his way across the ridges of the country. Never alone and never silent, and soon the sun will be shining on him again. A faint screaming begins. Clouds of game come out of the forests into the clearing, and this average member of the young herd stands there motionless, uncomprehending in his brightness, which also seems to attract other vermin. Michael stands there, affably charged, a live wire. He is at home and his own keeper. The woman weeps at his door, her heart is pounding like a wild thing. Her senses are put out because they are having to put in overtime yet again. Her senses are out of tune in the open, in these temperatures. Almost at the same time, the woman's circulation, overloaded with alcohol, collapses, and she sags in a heap by the door. Manure on a frozen bed. By day the lifts thread by in skeins, affording access to the landscape, and people meet and fall upon other people, unloving. This woman, never will she properly feel at home on this earth. A little human feeling trickles into the bushes, too. Scandalous.

By day they plunged through the uneven terrain, the sporting folk, but now, when they might be needed, there isn't a single one to be seen, to hold back this woman from her assault on herself, take her by the heart, and stop her wheels. Generally the Direktor regulates the financial current in his company, he flows into its channelled bed and then, at one with his member, produces a perfectly respectable stream of his own. He sees to it that the water is drained off as he wishes and through his senses. The married couple are currently in the shadow of houses, trees, night. Gerti hammers at the pitiless door and has already slipped down it. She kicks it. The student, without even having to do anything more, is worth any effort. He smiles and stays standing where he is. After all, Hermann is there, her man, her husband, whom he would never want to resemble. And this husband looks up, above him, where he is not accustomed to seeing anyone. The two men's gazes meet halfway, they are both motorized. Almost simultaneously, for a split second, they sense their bodies rebelling against death. Preventively, Michael lowers his gaze by one or two tiny degrees. They have both heard the crashing of waves in the shell of Gerti's cunt, that's all there is to it. No point in flailing their arms, only to be shifted a few derisory centimetres off balance by the propeller of lusts that, tinkling and crystal, set a wind blowing at head height. At least one of them doesn't find it worthwhile moving his expensive clothes just for the sake of this woman's will. The young man lights a cigarette, seeing he's bearing the flame in his hand anyway, chained to his ski slope, standing there and hearing the mountain birds of prey swish about him.

They are out to pluck the last little flame from his lighter, to take it to the humans below him, who feel closer to God than he does. He doesn't care either way about the fire in the village, he doesn't have to take it there. Gerti has escaped the vortex of the stove, where things spatter and crackle nicely too. But now it's enough, it is time she was taken and set, this precious gem in the Direktor's home. Examining her closely, the Direktor takes her by the waist and begins to drag her across the nighttime ground, touched with hoarfrost. She stamps and kicks her hooves, that's the last straw! She is still wearing the silk dress she had on this morning, in which hopes were aroused, and from the front and rear, Gerti's figure being what it is, things are looking good, even though it is as if the day, weighted with snow, were starting to sag a little. The student is simply not a giving man, nor will he ever be one. He looks out, shading his eyes, but there is not enough light to present the couple in glory. He does not always spurn the unfamiliar. After all, he did make a try at striding out brazenly over the fields, annoying the game, breathing the air and then returning it, used, to the piste. Still, it doesn't reach much further out into the landscape, his shining aura. Nonetheless, it can supply a frame for this holy family and the card-format view that includes them. Michael shades his eyes to let them grow used to the dark. Nature is not gentle, Nature is savage, and people fleeing from its emptiness take refuge in each other, of all places, where someone else is already in occupation. Perhaps Michael will go for a drink with the Direktor, who would like to finish the picture Michael started with his own stupid brush, the little prick. Amid the firs you no longer need language. Let's just throw it away!

Silence sweeps the streets, and God transfigures the inmates of the region — indeed, several of them are still at work, some carving and snippeting at their furniture and homes, the rest looking after their current partners

who are in non-permanent residence. New ones are
forever having to be hauled home (and promptly their
usefulness is at an end) to make Nature's standing
promise of work and shelter come true. At long last they
settle down! And so they keep the promises Nature
mistakenly gave them: the gentle blunders that became
human beings; and human errors have destroyed the
forests that give them life, too. One further thing that
Nature promised: the right to work, according to which
every occupier who has sealed a pact with his employer
can be delivered by death from God too (God's stinking
delivery). Now I've made a slip as well. Nor do the lords
of the land know of any deliverance from the dilemma.
There is less and less work, there are more and more
people doing everything they can to see it stays that way
and to see that they themselves stay. Like now, wearily
but proudly hanging their signs of life on the wall and
handing in their cards. All around, bodies are beginning
to develop, and the most oddly constructed of figures are
coming into existence. If the architect who made these
motorway-users could see the freaks arising flushed
with hope from their crumpled marital beds (to think of
all the other things they've crumpled!), he would
promptly redesign them, given that he himself rose
again in a far more thrilling way from his cramped
sepulchre to set us all an example, which can be studied
in museums and churches. The bad witness we all bear
the creator simply by being there and not being able to
help it: now they are all stirring and humming, and as
their bodies work they move in the rhythm of pop music
on the Ö3 station or a simple record. How calmly Marx
responded to us! All the spendthrift debts which they are
now collecting, hugging each other tight: who would
give them anything at this hour! Not even the innkeeper
by the bridge, obeying his dark instinct to earn more
than he has spent in the way of drinks, trying the food he
himself has prepared, where 86-year-old kitchen maid
Josefa licks the plates clean and gobbles up the leftovers.

Something is always left over of the work, to which they are more devoted than to their dearest beloved. The women have been freshly prepared, or preserved. Yes, they too desire something, but not for much longer, the way they're roaring under the lash of the weather, which even dictates their attire. Thus their round fat bodies hum away, life goes on, man vanishes continually in death, the hours sink to the ground, but women flit nimbly about the house, never safe from all the blows that fate deals. How alike their habits are! Every day it's the same. Tomorrow, tomorrow. Procrastination, procrastination! But the next day has not yet come, the woman of the house cannot yet enter it, to be finished off by yet more work. Now they repose unfeelingly in each other, the pistons thrust down, a course is set for the pathless shores of bodies but the goal is missed, yes, we may fall but we do not fall a long way down, we are as shallow as the shallowness about us. If our deserts went by what we earn, we would just be able to buy ourselves some shoes for our weary wanderers' feet, but no more, and already our partners are lapping about our ankles, they want to play themselves and think they are trumps, oh horror, they really are winning the trick! And the distance to the heavens remains ever the same. Quick, let's place a foot on the runner-board of the car, which we have wrested from our bodies in the form of work, many many hours put in at the factory. We have entered as children of God, and after many a year nothing remains but to board the cheapest of mid-market cars, and we whose gears have meanwhile changed slightly are refused access to the works by a master of shifts who newly holds the stick. Right, they have eliminated our place of work entirely, and now the factory operates almost on its own, it learnt it all from us! But before poverty moves in and the car is sold, let us ourselves come back a time or two from foreign parts. Let us squander ourselves in someone else's parts a time or two more. We will not be driven away from this table by any thought that has eluded our possessor, nor by any suit advertising in the newspaper, any nonsense to put a prompt stop to our lives because we poor work-horses absolutely had to have a few more horsepower in our meadow. And then there's the Direktor: he is not the sole ruler by any means! Not even the firm, that captive buzzard, can soar as it would. Who knows what other beast it might encounter!

Thus we all have our worries: whom we could love and what we could eat.

One would not imagine for a moment that there was anything fake about their feelings. Rather, one would think they were genuine jewels that others bedeck themselves with: the throngs of thonged bodies, tricked out in their best (new shoes!) and wandering the paths of their little love affairs, turning to a restless trick or two in their rooms. A human choir sending their many-voiced echo up unto the father in the air on the chair-lift. It was he who created the erogenous zones with which Woman pretties herself up of an evening, rapidly shoving her work out of sight lest anyone pay her properly. Flabbergasted, the men gape into their women's holes, torn by life, and yes, they shudder, as if they knew that the box has long been empty from which the seeds have been shaken out for years. But the dear women are so attached to them. And tomorrow morning the first bus has to be caught, no matter how helplessly they have to thrash their wives, who are attached to them and their short barrels: shoot! Jobs don't grow on trees.

The others, too, take this road to death. They accompany each other for a while, and breathe loudly at the gate, for it to be opened to them. And there come yet more people who have fallen into each other's weakly branches, to tangle their limbs. So that they are a twosome when they have to face their foreman. One has to be able to do something or other! To be bigger and more numerous would be a good start, if one is sinking beneath the stroke of the factory's daily scythe. And from the spoils the owners pick out the very best that you experienced this year on the beaches of Rimini and Carola, where, blooming luxuriantly, you sank beneath the rubble of your short-lived pleasures.

The Direktor of this factory drags his wife back to the car, meaning to shorten this short break by breaking a record at the work he understands best: words of love from his transmitter sound in her ear, and she receives them thrashing and stammering as loving couples without a stereo receive their dance music after mid-night. The window, where we can see one of those brightly coloured tracksuits such as generally fetch up in day-trip bars for filling, remains obstinately lit up. The young man stretches out his sleeves, gathered in at the ends with strong knitted cords, and stares out at these charmless people, who are nonetheless perfect in their way if one considers their income from the toil of humankind and their influence on state parliament politics. How wonderful to sing together with the rich and still not have to be in their works choir! To learn their ways and still not have to stand in the fields and have one's hair cut at harvest time! Like lumbering oxen the two cars are grazing side by side in front of the house, and one of the animals is now going to be disembowelled. The door opens, the light goes on. Words of endearment are sent to Gerti's home parts. This paterfamilias has not come to punish but to comfort and to resume possession, already there is a gleam as of a city beyond his gates. He has no desire but for his wife, who is sufficient unto him, unlike others who cannot stop making modest demands and singing and saying which of the photos in the relevant publications they prefer. How busily they bustle about at their sexual enterprises after work! And just take a look what these pikes in carp ponds have caught: it seems to me that at times Nature is inclement. The Direktor is attached to his wife. Her broad thoroughfares are familiar to him. And while the silent inmate of the home is still suspended in mid-air with his nice motorbike catalogue beyond the window, the Direktor slaps Gerti across the front seats (having first had to push a button, I won't say which), yanks her dress over her head and masters her buttocks so that, via her dirty and off-limits route, he can penetrate her interior. Tenderly hands knead the udder. A friendly tongue licks into an ear. This has often been done in the past, for people like to build a house beside one that is already there, not to support their neighbour but to torment. It is a little uncomfortable, true, summer is far off, the road is remote, the animals taste good, and everyone comes to the appointed places or at least is collected in the box not far away. This crashing surf can surge upon one as if in one's sleep, and hide on a raised look-out in the midst of Nature. Below, in the shimmer of the field glasses, the allied members liaising between work, money and the powerful who don't like to be alone, are flitting about. They forever have to lie on one another against one another. Human activity resumes with new aims, the weather is cold, and every time the Direktor withdraws his sturdy prick a little he casts a forceful glance at his silent admirer at the window. He only has to go through a slight contortion to do so. Perhaps the young man will cop a handful now as well! As far as I can tell, he's really doing it. From the waist down, we men are all members of the same club, when all's said and done. That is, our members belong to our women and in the street we allow fate to be pressed into our hands without offering resistance. Let us make ourselves comfortable in each other! Michael has his hand down the front of his tracksuit trousers, I think, and is cramming his clothing full of himself. And Gerti's dress is now completely unbuttoned too and her bags and pouches are flopping out, if you'll pardon my mentioning it. Never mind, even if the Direktor's feeling the draught, within himself he pays attention to festiveness and quality, we forgive him. Face forward, the woman is squashed into the car upholstery, as if slumber lay concealed in these leather shadows. Her legs dangle to left and right out of the open door. And her husband, this bellowing native of the country, to whom we have entrusted our homeland for him to make paper out of it (the trees would have been condemned to a close shave anyway), he is far more at home here than we could ever be! I hear this bird shouting as he sings. He slips to Gerti's side and rams several of his loving fingers inside her. He speaks in friendly tones to her, describing the winners she still stands to score. Then he drives into her hole again with a crash. Briefly he withdraws and feels up his sceptre: as we see, his pace is unmeasured and immoderate. Now the woman is being examined by an expert who is harnessing his energy under the bonnet and sending his little salesman off, indeed, even accompanies him in person, we'll manage this, no problem, and then lock up afterwards.

Gerti's secrets have long been revealed, her closed doors are wide open, now she's dealt a few blows on her behind and back, that's how friends deal with each other, that way there's no mistake. The Direktor also drives the vehicle of his tongue in, who shall interpret that for us? A number of young village men have taken up their posts at the posterns of naked women and are hoping to be considered when posts are assigned. They want to collect but not pay. Their wives help them with their immortality and with the high mortality rate of their work. But the Direktor goes his own hot way alone. Everyone is familiar with his still youthful radiance. The woman, commingled with him in disorder, now has to put up with him in her arse, there may be any number of paths and some may be better surfaced too. While other people are at the mercy of disease, this lordandmaster is serving himself with equanimity at his usual counter, where his child came from too, right next door. No need to be afraid, his member is safe there. Now the excited animal goes for a trot in the woman where it has been taken in order to grow. It catches slightly in the chain it has torn loose, the calf. And so it stands stock still till it's shot down. The familiar trampling and traipsing has already worn the woman badly. Never mind, there's a good cream for everything and a cash present. Grease well and you get ahead better. And soon fresh greenery will be coming up for the man to pull out.

What a divine group, though soon they'll have to take a rest. Body to body, they are a threat to each other. Whimpering after a number of further slips, the Direktor collapses limp upon his wife, who was so well-appointed. He has reaped her high-yield region thoroughly, it has his recommendation, and now there won't be any fodder growing there in a hurry. His river shoots wrathfully out of him, and from the labourers who are presented to them on golden platters their gods and personnel bosses seize the share that is yours by force. Go on, choose the best from a wide assortment too, and see: you already have it at home, call it your better half and leave her doing the washing-up and scrubbing and sweating!

This time the Direktor is in valid order and his wife is satisfied. But tomorrow he may be running riot again, shooting from the hip and buying any ticket at all to who knows where. At least his wife is still protected and desired, though, there are so many paths to be taken, after all, to the theatre, a concert, a season ticket to the opera, opportunity enough to lick the thing which the Direktor reaches across with a whimper and wrap it up anew. Now he has turned her onto her back and is wagging about in her face. A thin thread of slobber dribbles down, and promptly the meatloaf and sauce is brought to the woman's lips, a soft tired suckling. Mmm, that's just perfect. She is requested to clean away what she has brought from the kitchen for presentation and thawing. First the banks, then the shaft, neat and tidy, all the tiny creases as well, after all there's a little driving still to be done today and we wouldn't want this quick-acting foam all over the upholstery. And then Gerti is expected to kiss the hairy scrotum, mind your eyes. As if he were stripping a snake, the Direktor rips the dress off his wife with a single tear, though at the same time whispering that tomorrow she will get two new ones to replace it. The dress is forcefully pulled apart at the front. Gerti's body is kissed from a convenient height and then belted into the seat again, where it remains caught, returning none of the looks bestowed on it. The Direktor goes on to rip Gerti's petticoat too, exposing her entire dilapidated façade; soon, albeit outside, beyond the battered attaché cases, pleasant green will be appearing, one or two months of the yoke still to go! Let the airstream and the one or two stray people returning home take a look at the building if they want, in the warm shadows of which the Direktor has been sporting. The woman does not resemble any film actress, at least none I know of. It is quiet. Michael peers out of the window and makes an effort to grow once again in order to make the most and best of himself. Not everyone has a handsome member to amuse himself with. The Direktor is faithful by nature, that's how it should be. We are the hearth of the household and warm the lordsandmasters if necessary.

The young man, thinking of the countless friends whom he will make the repositories of his adventure, steps under the too needling waterjet of the shower. His senses are all present and stretch out on the floor like dogs lying down to sleep on their appointed blankets. Perhaps his girlfriend will stop by later on, while outside the oppressed take by force what has been granted them. Thus long he has deigned to watch a woman advancing in years, and thus long will he rest, a child of the world. I think he will even still be asleep tomorrow morning when the people who live in these houses trample each other to death in the bus and riotously batter each other about the head with their belongings.

As if by changing cars they had changed lives, the Direktor and his wife drive home together, one under the protection of the other, tossing from one position in life to the next. These people can fuck fearlessly anywhere at all, whatever they do is always put right again by love and their dear cleaning ladies. The employees are at rest, presently the jangle of their alarms will raise them aloft. Silently the car sweeps the flatland clean. The mountains stand in silence, till tomorrow the sun is again portioned out by the tourist office rep, to delight the sporting folk. And so the directorial couple return home on their great raft, along the federal highway in accordance with all the regulations and at a moderate speed. For a brief while the two of them took hold on their bodies to fill up with fuel, the springs were bubbling up all around them, right, the rich tank up new energy as often as they wish. In the little houses silence reigns, because the people there have to count out the money for petrol first. At most it's violence that reigns, till tomorrow they are under someone else's control again at the factory, these sons from petty homes, and their wives wade by day through the puddles of the powerful sex. Love comes fruity and fresh in its carton, but what does it become inside us?

The toil of the sexes, accomplished today by the Direktor and the Frau Direktor, has made them blossom with a shudder, only to wipe their mouths afterwards as if after a meal wolfed greedily down; and it may be but is not definitely finished for today. Till we meet again tomorrow in the radiant light from the mail van's headlamps, so early, when it's still dark, not to mention the years ahead! Nothing but those lights caresses the wretched bodies shamelessly confronting us in all their morning stench and exhaust fumes. But just think of the lottery tickets their thoughts are always dwelling on! One has to be able to take it as well as deal it out.

The Direktor stammers managerial, loving words, he announces himself and his programme, this private individual. Already he is in his element again: money. What would he be without his wife, as he insists on calling her. Jovially he embraces her with the arm he's not steering with, taking her body and doing some steering there at least. Like a warm tame animal the mountains lounge above him, he has already sheered them quite bald. They have left the superfluous car standing, put to sleep and locked up like their child. Let's face it, all they were thinking of was jolly sex. The woman can now go shopping for the kind of commodities that suit a woman. Now speculations are made concerning the next day and what it might bring. The Direktor describes the many and various ways in which he is going to screw his wife later and in the days ahead. He needs trouble up top, in the office, if his prick down below is to be satisfied and taken captive by the woman. Perhaps the woman will like something special which she will follow blindly on her shopping spree tomorrow? This man: the unwavering star of his wife will shine above him till tomorrow morning, he nuzzles tenderly at her throat, keep your eyes on the road, don't look away! The droplets fly from the man, sweat and sperm, which makes him no less, no slighter, no smaller. Smilingly he prays to his wife, whom he has held under his jet. His fleshy testicles sit still on their stringy stalk. What a relief, to go out into the spell of night, if one doesn't have to hurry out into the morning dark, one amongst many, dazzled by the kitchen light. If the fire is burning within one, and another, larger one is burning in the engine. Cleansed and renewed, the Direktor will presently be

getting into bed again with his Gerti and making his
territorial mark on her bush, no one cocks a leg faster
than he does. Maybe the two of them will once again be
flooded by the muted cry of their bodies wanting food,
who knows? The woman tries to fasten her dress at her
breast, the cold is scourging her. But the man demands
that she provide a little more entertainment for him and
the people who live in those parts in their little domestic
limbos, please, Brigitte, I mean, Gerti. The dress, which
is covering her now, he parts wide open again, she hasn't
quite gone out yet, hasn't Gerti, I'm pretty sure there's
still a glimmer in the ashes. The heating hasn't properly
warmed up yet, but the man has. He is fast off the mark,
on his chin he has a fingernail scratch dealt by Gerti. Not
a single walker comes their way, to flower a little with an
acquaintance outside the house. No one is out and about
any more to witness the brand of power on the forehead
of the factory Direktor. And so he at least has to stamp
his mark on his wife, to show that she has paid to go in
and really did bravely go out in the open from the
warmth of her sex. In the kitchens of the poor, only the
stove is kept alight.

The man calls the woman his darling, and yes, even the
child is included. They live in the centre, the happy
medium, the gusset of the village. And the government
shrewdly ladles out the special offers to people. So that
the owners of companies can take their decisions and
come up with excuses for squandering subsidies and
human bodies. They can be happy forever amid their
possessions, and the rest tell of worries on their towel-
sized patches of ground where they promptly plant out
fences, despite the fact that their seed is scarcely enough
for more than two. Already they have to be thinking of
yet another person!

We are there, the child is asleep in his private parts and
memories.

Meekly the son slumbers on the lead of Linz Chemicals Ltd. Now let us go to sleep as well, for a foretaste of what comes before death. To do this one first has to lie down, as the poor have long known, they die sooner too, and still the time till they die seems too long to them. The Man nuzzles up once more to the cosmetically caked skin of his wife, presently he will follow her into bed with a bang, like a shot from a gun. In the bathroom there is already a busy noise of waters and movements. Mercilessly a heavy body is thrown into the hot water to make it fit for consumption. The soap and brushes lie on his chest. The mirrors steam up. The Frau Direktor is expected to give her husband's back a good scrubbing, to dip her hand acquiescently into the lather and go on massaging his massive sex, it is entirely in her hands. Beyond the window, the moon slithers. He is already calling for her, the Man and the half kilo of flesh (or, if need be, less) which is his master. Already it is swelling again in the warm water and arising to lord it over the lavish cold buffet of his body. Afterwards he will bathe the woman after the troubles of the day, not at all, his pleasure entirely. All around, mortals are living on wages and work, they do not live for ever and they do not live well. But now they have exchanged their tribulations for rest, the sting is asleep in their breast because they do not have their own bathroom. The Direktor's body just goes in the water, but he still has enough cubic metres of solid flesh left. Once again he calls for his wife, louder this time, it is an order. She does not come. He will have to soften up all by himself in the water. Placidly he slides across to the other side of the tub, should he yell for her to come? How pleasant that water does not change one, and that one does not have to learn to walk on it. Such a pleasure, and so cheap. Anyone can afford it. Let the woman stay where she is, oh take me with you, swathes of heat! He runs the hot tap, massages it and feels peaceful, serene. The waters rush about his heavy body, the hard jaw muscles grinding life up small and swallowing companies. The poor too fall like water from the cliffs, but at least they stay where they are, in their little beds, and don't go begging constantly, these tedious people wanting danger money paid. One moment all's well, and the next, complete with all the sacred strings their wives have laboriously stretched on their bodily frames, they're blindly getting caught in the machines! All that blood! And all for nothing, including in the end the massive whiplash beating of their hearts, since there is no more blood left to keep them going. And I gather the children are sometimes still out and about at four in the morning. One or two of them, at least, still come home drunk from the disco.

But his son, unpopular here for so many years already, is lying in bed, and the placid moon passes on. He is breathing heavily, the boy, and is bathed in a cold sweat. With tablets of that kind in his juice, his sleep is altogether different. Comfortless he lies there under the eye of his mother, who comes to his bed and smooths the covers. The boy is flaccid and yet he is her whole world: he is silent, and so is her world. He is no doubt looking forward to growing up, like his father's member. Tenderly Mother kisses her little boat sailing around the world. Then she takes a plastic bag, slips it over the boy's head, and draws it tight at the bottom so that the child's breath will perish in peace. Under the tent of the back, on which is printed the address of a boutique, the boy's life force burgeons richly one more time, this boy to whom not long ago growing-up and sports gear were promised. That's how it goes when one tries to improve on Nature with mechanical implements! But no, the child still wants to live. Then the son drifts out into the open waters where he is immediately quite in his element (Mummy!) and uses the snorkel mask through which his fellows learn to see the world, as if through goo, from the very start: so utterly was he their boss, a little god of war, at work, rest and play. They see everything, yet they do not see much. Mother leaves the house. She is carrying her son in her arms like a budding cutting that has to be planted. From the mountaintops where the boy went sledging today and was planning to go again tomorrow (to be exact, the next day has already been impatiently begun on!), the earth bids its farewell. Outrageous imprints in the blanket of snow. Sure, go wandering about near the fire if you will: quite an experience, eh?

The mother carries the child, and then, when she grows tired, drags him along behind her. Discreetly clad in moonlight. Now the woman is at the stream, and the next moment her son sinks in, contented. Perfect peace is beckoning, and sporting people beckon and wave to each other at every opportunity too, if there's an audience. Now, contrary to expectation, it has turned out to be the youngest of the family who will be permitted to see the stupid face of eternity first, behind all the money that runs about at liberty on the earth, for purchases, if no one puts it on a lead. People compete in races, the events are thunderous but they don't want rain. And skiers go into the mountains, never mind who else lives there and might like to win themselves.

The water has taken hold of the child, and bears him on and away, a good deal will remain of him for a long time in this cold. The mother is alive, her time is wreathed and limited, with fetters she has twined in it. Women age early, and their mistake is not knowing where to hide all the time that lies behind them so that no one sees it. What are they to do, devour it like the umbilical cords of their children? Hell and damnation!

But now rest a while!

The Piano Teacher

Translated by Joachim Neugroschel

Erika Kohut teaches piano at the Vienna Conservatory by day.
But by night she trawls the porn shows of Vienna while her
mother, whom she loves and hates in equal measure, waits up
for her.

Into this emotional pressure-cooker bounds music student and
ladies' man, Walter Klemmer. With Walter as her student, Erika
spirals out of control, consumed by the ecstasy of self-
destruction.

First published in 1983, *The Piano Teacher* is the masterpiece of
Elfriede Jelinek, Austria's most famous writer. Directed by
Michael Haneke, the film won three major prizes at the
Cannes 2001 Festival, including best actor for Benoît Magimel
and best actress for Isabelle Huppert.

'A disturbing tale of love, fear and self-destruction . . . in this
demented love story, the hunter is the hunted, pain is pleasure,
and spite and self-contempt seep from every pore' *The
Guardian*

'Draws its disturbing power from what it says about female
sexuality' *Sunday Herald*

'A bravura performance, translated into vivid, flowing
colloquial American-English, in which . . . the bleak landscape
is lit by flashes of irony' Shena Mackay

'A brilliant, deadly book' Elizabeth Young